E. C. Cornell

Eighty Years Ashore and Afloat or The Thrilling adventures of Uncle Jethro

Embracing the remarkable Episodes in a Life of Toil and Danger, on Land and Sea

E. C. Cornell

Eighty Years Ashore and Afloat or The Thrilling adventures of Uncle Jethro
Embracing the remarkable Episodes in a Life of Toil and Danger, on Land and Sea

ISBN/EAN: 9783743422421

Manufactured in Europe, USA, Canada, Australia, Japa

Cover: Foto ©Andreas Hilbeck / pixelio.de

Manufactured and distributed by brebook publishing software (www.brebook.com)

E. C. Cornell

Eighty Years Ashore and Afloat or The Thrilling adventures of Uncle Jethro

Eighty Years Ashore and Afloat,

OR THE

THRILLING ADVENTURES OF UNCLE JETHRO.

Embracing the remarkable Episodes in a life of
Toil and Danger, on Land and Sea,

BY

E. C. CORNELL.

BOSTON:
ANDREW F. GRAVES,
20 CORNHILL.

TO THE

BRAVE AND GENEROUS

WHO HAVE NOBLY BREASTED THE OCEAN BILLOWS,

THIS BOOK

IS RESPECTFULLY DEDICATED,

BY THEIR FRIEND,

E. C. CORNELL.

V

CONTENTS.

7

Eighty Years Ashore and Afloat,

OR

THRILLING ADVENTURES OF UNCLE JETHRO.

CHAPTER I.

INTRODUCTORY.

THE writer of the following narrative, having often listened with no slight degree of interest to the stories of an old man, feeling desirous that others may enjoy their recital, after mature reflection has given himself to the attempt of combining them in one volume ; fully believing that if it does not possess so much of the marvellous or supernatural as works emanating only from the imagination of the novelist, yet it may be no less wonderful when properly regarded as a truthful narrative of episodes in the life and experience of one who is still able to give us the facts ("that

9

are stranger 'than fiction ") from his own lips. As it
is not our intention to give to the work an independent preface, and claiming for ourself no merit as a
professional scribbler, permit us to say that even the
contemplation of preparing such a work for the public
scrutiny has given us many misgivings. Often the
idea has been strangled, e'er its conception was per-
fected, but finally, regardless of the jeers and rebukes
of unfriendly critics, we enter upon the duties involved,
imparting to it (at least) the benefits of integrity and
truthful delineation, which it is hoped will enhance its
value, or make it prolific in interest to those who scan
its pages. The subject who will figure most conspic-
uously in this narrative is allowed the privilege of in-
troducing himself, as best suited to his own good taste
and judgment.

> Now lend an ear, both young and old,
> As tales quite strange we shall unfold,
> Of life, in years almost fourscore
> Lived by one man on sea and shore.

Or in other words, let us listen to what *Uncle Jethro*
has to say.

CHAPTER II.

WELL boys, I tell you what it is, if you say go ahead, go ahead it shall be. If correctly informed I was born in a small hamlet, on the outskirts of the village of Edgartown. My parents were not, what at the present time would be considered wealthy, but enjoying the reputation of respectability; and as "a good name is better than great riches," they should have felt rich (especially after I was born),—which incident happened in the earlier part of my life, so long ago in fact, that to me the particulars attending that important occasion are almost obliterated. Trusting, however, to the family record, it was the year of grace, 1793, that bequeathed to society an ornament. destined to appear upon the mantle-piece of the nation. ⋅ For the information of individuals not familiar with our exact location, let me tell you that Edgartown, the shire town of the County of Dukes, situated on the southern extremity of the, to-day, far-famed island of Marthas Vineyard (without its celebrated "Oak Bluffs." and "Highlands," its "Bellevue," -"Sunset," and "Ocean" heights, its "Look-out Mountain" and

11

" Katama "), is only remembered as a small and sparse-ly-populated village, the principal occupation of its in-habitants being the catching of fish, of the different kinds and dimentions, with which its neighboring waters were abundantly supplied. Here ai d there might have been seen among its places of business the shop of a Hatter, Blacksmith and Cooper ; a few signs significant of the fact that West India goods were for sale,—coffies, spices and oils, not forgetting rum, gin and brandy, articles of commerce at that early period very neces-sary, especially the last-mentioned. For to be without these, let it be remembered, was like the Irishman going to be married and depending upon the magistrate to furnish the bride. A number of wharves graced the shores of the inner harbor (which it is not boasting to say is one of the finest on the American continent) as many a sailor has found to his great joy, when enabled to drop anchor there after buffeting the bitter blasts of a wintery storm. Besides the many vessels of dif-ferent grades and nationalities that frequently were seen swinging at anchor between the opposite shores of Chappaquiddic and our own, not unfrequently a ship or lighter craft, principally owned on the island of Nantucket, would be brought here for the purpose of being fitted for a whaling voyage, — an occurrence at-taching to the village, an importance not to be lightly regarded. As my narrative progresses I may have oc-casion to refer to the whaling interest, for to a great degree are the financial resources of our island attributed to the success attending the whale-fishing. And here it may not be out of place to state that the Vineyard has furnished commanders for more ships engaged in that business, (since the time of the opening of our story), than the same population in any other part of the globe.

In the early period, of which I have been speaking, it was not customary for boys to spend a great portion of time at school, and even were the facilities offered it was not deemed essential to the happiness of the rising generation to make any advances beyond the literary attainments of the fathers. If enabled to handle a sail or take a trick at steering, it was an accomplishment useful indeed, if not quite as ornamental, as was often realized during the hazardous voyages which comprised much of my subsequent life. At the age of eighty years, my much revered father's death cast its shadows over our happy household. To be thus early in life deprived of the love and care which only a parent can bestow, was illy calculated to lighten the burdens of youth, or make the future to me more bright or hopeful. As troubles never come singly, it was deemed prudent that our family be represented. Accordingly a situation was soon procured, which resulted in giving me a home (if entitled to so endearing a name), in the family of my uncle, who was a sour and crusty specimen of human frailties, apparently taking delight in every conceivable manner to impress upon me its unwholesome fruits, which if not deservedly measured out, rather tended for the time being to appease an unhallowed disposition, at the same time, doubtless, endowed me with the iron will and constitution that my future career was destined to require. By nature a modest lad, somewhat sensitive withal. I was easily provoked, — not always strictly in accordance with the teachings of the Bible, "to good works," but more in unison with the disturbed and turbulent feelings which the training of a hard master constantly instilled within me.

Passing over a few years (the memory of which presents no silver lining, and, from the absence of incident, interesting or instructive to no one), I come to a more active period in my life, leaving conjecture to supply the interim, with the assurance that whatever of hard lines the imagination may portray, the picture will not be overdrawn. At the age of twelve years, I find myself chief mate of the two-masted Schooner Jay, of twenty tons burden, commanded by my guardian who was owner, sailing-master, and all hands, excepting myself, who, as has already been said, held, the responsible and honorable position of mate, the duties of which office, from my experience along shore in open boat, fishing &c., I felt perfectly qualified to perform. Though small of stature, my healthy condition of body, as well as natural aptitude of mind made up the deficiency of my insignificant proportions and neglected education.

CHAPTER III.

ABOUT the middle of July, 1804, very early in the morning was snugly lying, in the quiet, and placid waters of the southern or upper part of the harbor, a neat little craft. Her rigging was set up tight, and the silver beams of the moon glistening upon the newly painted hull and spars, indicated to the observer that a voyage was contemplated. The vessel was almost land-locked, by a point making out, dividing the waters of Katama Bay from our harbor coming in close proximity with a point reaching out from the shore opposite, making it a very desirable location for safety, even in the worst weather. This place was called "The Swimming place," doubtless from its being frequently used for the purpose of swimming cattle from one island to the other. It was on board of this vessel that I was ordered to put the cargo, ready for shipment. My boyish imaginations as fancy pictured the prospective voyage, imparted an excitement to the occasion long to be remembered, and the cargo consisting of quahaugs, oil, fish, and wool, was

16

soon taken in and securely stowed away, when I reported ready for sea. The Captain soon after came on board accompanied by two ladies, who sought passage for New Haven, where we were to market our goods. All on board, sail was soon made, our moorings loosed, and with a fair and gentle breeze our home and native village receded from our view; which, as I had time to reflect upon it, cast a slight shade of sadness on my heart. For, let it be remembered, it was the first time leaving the spot endeared to me by many pleasant memories, and a short voyage, even, at that early period, in so diminutive a craft as our own, was considered quite an undertaking, while the daring spirits accomplishing it were looked upon as almost kindred to old Neptune himself.

During the passage, which proved exceedingly pleasant, nothing worthy of note occurred, if we except an occasional glimpse of the bright eyes of our lady passengers, as they appeared from the cabin gang-way, and a little fright of which the captain was the innocent cause. On the night of the first day out, the Captain took the early watch on deck, calling me at twelve. The wind was dead aft, quite moderate, and instructing me to keep off all I could without gibing he repaired to the cabin. The shores of Connecticut were on our starboard beam; the wind canting more to the southward, I kept off, and by so doing obeyed orders and ran on a ledge of rocks. Finally beating over, escaped without further damage than giving our passengers a fright from which they did not wholly recover until safely landed on the wharf at New Haven. After the exchange of friendly wishes and parting salutations, our sails were furled and the deck cleared for business. From sailors we very soon became merchants, and when we had exchanged our chattels for fruit, both from our deck and sometimes using a pedler's wagon, scouring the country for purchasers and in return taking country produce, we very soon found ourselves in readiness to return. Nantucket being considered the best place to dispose of our goods, we went thither, found a ready market, and in less than ten days from the day of our departure dropped anchor at home. Beside acting as chief mate; I was also cook and attended to the preparation of the table generally.

Now we are ready to make up another cargo or freight, which is principally done by catching fish, including the bivalves, or, as sometimes a good opportunity offers, they are purchased at a low figure and disposed, of in the manner already mentioned. Making five or six cruises through the season. I continued in this business during that and the following Summer, not always, however, going to the same place for customers. It was on one of these cruises that I received from the hands of my faithful guardian the last infliction of his wrath. And when it occurs to memory, I can scarce suppress my laughter as still I seem to behold him in the unenviable plight my unrestrained passion placed him, when forced to the conclusion that the time had fully come when good nature, or endurance, "ceased to be a virtue." I do not remember just what I had done to arouse his anger, nor did it always need a pretext to insure, what he considered a punishment; for sometimes I judged, he would punish tor fear I might need it at some future time. Be that as it may, it was while lying along side a wharf in Boston, after disposing of a load and ready to return homeward. It was Sunday morning. Calling me aft, with the end of the draw-bucket rope he commenced to administer upon me in a way not at all pleasing to myself, nor gratifying to the bystanders gazing with wonder and amazement from the pier above, and arguing the case with him. No moral effect being attainable as I was able to discern, I told him, clenching my fists, that if he gave me another blow I didn't know but I would be the death of him. He still appeared undismayed, when quickly catching the rope attached to the well filled bucket of grease and water, giving it a tremendous jerk, I wholly disqualified him to attend church with any degree of decency, as his light, tight pants strongly represented some dish-cloths when hung up to dry. While with him, after that time he treated me more humanely, and when I left him to make other and longer voyages we separated in a friendly manner.

CHAPTER IV.

ESIDES our usual cargo, we had two gentlemen passengers, a man and a boy, both from the rural districts of Connecticut. They came in search of health along the shores of the Vineyard, showing good sense there, if they did not in anything else. Had been absent from home since the Monday previous,(it now being Friday),and you can judge how very desirous they were of returning after such a separaation, as also our active measures to facilitate their wishes. As readily assumed, seamanship had not been to any extent embraced in the culture or education of our cabin occupants, if they manifested a disposition to remain in it, in preference to appearing on deck they certainly were excusable, even though the circumstances of the case required, for their own safety, what aid or assistance they might render.

Starting with a fair wind, we soon entered Vineyard Sound, but the weather changing, and a thick fog coming in, we found it absolutely indispensable that we should put in to Tarpaulin Cove, a convenient re-

20

sort for wind-bound vessels, on the N. W. side of the Sound, bearing from Gay Head light nearly north. Here we were detained by a gale and dense fog for a number of days, which, from the loneliness and dreary aspect of the place, did not serve to keep us in the best of spirits. Fearful that our shellfish would suffer the consequences of our delay; it was decided that in case the weather would not permit us to prosecute the trip westward, to return home, and by putting them into their native element, prolong their vitality. Early the next morning made sail on our craft, the Captain ordering me to take the helm while he catheaded the anchor and cleared up deck. Ran out of the Cove, soon after discerning, through the fog, a ship on our weather bow. "Luff! Luff!" cried I, "in accents wild," as the vessel threatened to run us down. Hauling off to clear us, we foreclaid him, and hailing asked him if he wanted a pilot. Instantly heaving his yards back, he replied, (Yankee like,) by asking, "where are we now?" After giving the information sought, we found her to be the Boston-bound ship John Jay. The fog lifting, he preferred to keep on and procure a pilot after getting into Holmes Hole, thinking perhaps it could be done for a less sum than was required by our captain, viz.: forty dollars to be taken to the foot of Nantucket shoals. Hardly had he filled away when the fog again closed, perfectly obscuring the land, when rattle, rattle, went his blocks, and with

his yards the second time aback, he hailed us to send a
pilot to his relief, as he was shut up in the dark. As
the captain jumped into the boat to board, he instruct
ed me to follow the ship to the flats at the entrance
of our harbor, there to set a signal for help from shore
to get us in.

The fog thickened rather than diminished, while on
kept the ship, and by not being able to judge when to
alter my course, followed until too late to put back
Found we had passed Cape Pogue, and that we
were in a region of country (if the sea may be so
called,) where I was entirely unacquainted. What
could now be done ? was the question I asked myself
With the wind blowing a gale, it was my only chance
to still keep the ship in view, but for the safety of
the vessel and ourselves, sail must be reduced or we
should soon run under. An ugly sea, causing our lug
foresail to cut and slash in a terrible manner, demanded
immediate attention. I called for the passengers to
come and take the helm. At first they flatly refused
but after some naughty words, their fears of a watery
gave, which was eloquently portrayed, had the effect
of ·inducing the man to appear; and the assistance he
rendered doubtless made one less disaster at sea to be
recorded. The vessel being thus relieved, made better
weather. When I turned my eye to where the ship
was last observed, with dismay I found myself unable
to catch a glimpse of her. Now, thought I, we are in

for it. Whether she had kept on sailing, hauled aback, or changed her course, I was unable to determine ; and if alarm was not depicted on my usually placid countenance about that time, it never was in all my life. And vain it is to tell that the face is a true index to the emotions of one's heart. The fog apparently could be sliced with a case knife, like old cheese, which, from the emptiness of my stomach, having fasted since the previous night, was very suggestive of that same article and hard-tack in the locker below, it being the usual rations in bad times on board such craft.

Remembering the bearings of the ship when last seen followed in that direction, thinking that probably there were shoals in her way, which she would have to alter her course to avoid, and thus first bringing upon our own vessel, I could not with any degree of composure await the consequences. For I always had a dread of the water as a beverage, especially when taken in too large quantities, it generally giving me the stomach ache. I felt that my position was rather unenviable, every minute seemed an hour, and the almost distracted groans and cries of my companions, issuing from the cabin, did not have a tendency to tranquillize my own mind, or suggest any way of escape. In pity I endeavored to dispel the fears of the unfortunate landsmen by hiding my own as best I could, till gladdened by the ship heaving in sight, right ahead, with her sails clewed up, waiting for our approach Ascertain-

ing where we were, the ship gradually kept on. Afterwards did not lose sight of her until after going along
side and receiving our captain, who, after being paid
off, gave the commander of the ship the course from
Nantucket, bade him a prosperous passage and joined
our own craft again. He received for his services
forty-three dollars, overrunning the amount charged by
three .dollars, which I thought ought to have been
given to me. But my uncle "did not see it in that
light."

Hauling sharp on the wind, beat all that night and
till nearly dark, of the next day, when we ran safely
into our snug little harbor, and took out our shell-fish,
to recruit their energies Our passengers went up to
the old tavern, only too glad to tread *terra firma* once
more. They didn't care whether school kept or not.
One week after, we resumed the voyage with better
success, landing our passengers in safety, and, as before, disposing of. our freight to good advantage,
making a very profitable cruise, with the exception of
frightening me so decidedly that it required thirty
years of after life to regain my growth. Shortly after,
the schooner Betsey & Polly returning from a fishing
voyage up the Straits, with a cargo of salted fish, I
accepted the chance to cook for the party who were
employed to cure them, which was done at a place
called Pond Lot, where a gravelly beach was handy
for spreading, etc. In the Winter that followed, my

time was variously occupied ; more particularly in the eeling business, in which a great deal of jobbing is done, though not in those days requiring quite the muscle as at present, it being followed simply to satisfy the immediate demands of hunger, instead of furnishing an article of export.

Spring approaching, feeling that the recompense heretofore received was not according to the views of my ambition, I decided to ship on board some other craft, and carve out my fortune on my own hook. An opportunity soon presented, and the parties to whom my plans were made known, being acquainted with my abilities, were quite desirous to make me the offer of cook's berth, on board the standing topsail schooner Nancy, of 43 tons, bound to the coast of Labrador on a fishing expedition, under the command of Capt. Lot Norton, with a crew of eight men, beside myself, an account of which you shall have forthwith.

CHAPTER V.

UR small stores on board the schooner, the fishing tackle in apple-pie order, and the salt for
curing the fish we anticipated catching, in the
hold, with the wind south-west, we set sail in the morning of the first of May. A thick fog enveloped us,
but lifting as we came up with, or in the vicinity of
Nantucket Point, from which our departure was
made. For the five days following we were prevented by thick weather from getting an observation, strong
westerly and north winds prevaling. The schooner was
a terrible hard craft to steer, requiring almost the
strength of a Goliah to keep her under subjection,
and making rather uncertain at times the exact distance run or course followed. At night of the fifth
day out, our skipper remarked that at two o'clock
the next day his reckonings would be up, and we
should be ashore on Cape Race, Newfoundland, which
caused much uneasiness among the crew as they
were not desirous that the voyage should terminate
in just such a manner. At one o'clock, however, we
discovered right ahead of us two boats, which proved
to be fishermen from a vessel lying in the harbor of
Cape Race. Getting near enough, we hailed them and

inquired how soon they intended to go in. "We do not care how soon," was the reply. Upon being invited to come on board they immediately complied, smelling, no doubt, the glass of grog they expected to get, — this pleasing incident, in the recognized custom of those days, warranting such an indulgence. It did not prove an illusion of the brain ; the bottle was passed, and "a nipper all round" made us feel "as young as we used to be." So, finding that our calculations did not vary thirty minutes, to the honor of those who had the navigation of the vessel in charge the whole sail from our leaving port being accomplished in weather thick as mud. With the boats in tow, soon squared away for the harbor, where we found our neighbors and enjoyed with them a good "gam," imparting to them the latest home intelligence, and enjoying the short season together satisfactorily.

There is much of sameness in the experience of the Labrador fishermen, and writers have so often detailed those interesting cruises, that I will not weary you now with a recital of the full particulars relating to them. Suffice it to say, after remaining here two or three days, our course was continued; making the Bay of Islands for boats masts, wood &c., from there to Shallow Bay, remaining a while, then crossing the straits to a place called Dog Island, where our fishing commenced. Here we fell in with a number of our towns people, which gave the place an air of pleasantry as often we came together and talked of home and the loved ones. One day, in company with the boats of the topsail scooner Betsy and Polly, went out to try our luck. Moored our boats to a rock which pro- jected out of water, while the boats of the other vesels anchored off. We would talk and pass jokes very freely, until almost unconsciously to ourselves our boats were quite laden with fish; and by this time, too, a considerable swash was caused by the rising wind, which somewhat hastened our movements in letting go our moorings and regaining the vessel. It was not long before other boats were coming, but observing that there was one less than there was before on the fishing ground, from its absence it was feared that it had been swamped, which proved true. The occut pants of the lost boat were one white man and a deaf and dumb negro, both finding a watery grave, where no memorial will ever be erected to mark their last resting-place. Continued in this vicinity until the fish struck eastward, when we followed them, entering a harbor called Nancy Belong, hard by a village con- sisting of a few huts occupied by Canadians: both English and Americans having the right to cast line in these waters. Up to this time we had taken about six hundred quintal of cod fish, making them on the rocks at Brador Basin, and readily selling them at three dollars per quintal to vessels bound to the Mediterranean. We came home in ballast. Getting back as far as Bay of Islands, the wind came out ahead, blowing so hard that we made a harbor where we remained a few days. In some hurry to get home, and the wind lessening, thought to gain a little to windward. Hove short and got sail on her, making a long leg and a short one back. Being a remarkably dull sailor and the wind greatly increasing, it was soon discovered to be necessary to shorten sail. Heading her in shore, we fell to leeward of the port we had left, and in order to make a harbor which our safety demanded, were compelled to run dead to the leeward eighty miles! This was getting home with a vengance. "But such was life I often had been told. And found it even so while I've been growing old." The wind coming in our favor, we made another start and arrived off Halifax, when very suddenly a gale even more severe than the first threatened to give us an opportunity of paying our compliments personally to Davy Jones. We hove to under close sail, and the wind began to slacken, finally dying away to a calm, the old swell causing us to rock fearfully. The deck watch thought best to call all hands for the purpose of getting enough sail on her to steady her. The call was made, but before they had time to get upon deck, a heavy roll to windward brought us just right to let a sea board us, taking off quarter rails, stanchions, and completely sweeping the decks smashing in the dead-lights, staving the boats, and breaking things generally.

The cabin was almost filled with water, and the men
on deck only saved themselves by clutching the tiller
and crutch-ropes aft. We soon made sail, cleared the
wreck, and with a moderate breeze, after a tedious
passage of forty days, arrived in Boston, getting our
drafts honored at mercantile houses of that city. Then
deturned to Edgartown where the vessel was refitted
by Capt. T. Jernegan, a merchant of some reputation
and a citizen of the place. Thus ended my first voyage
to sea, and my share of the proceeds amounted to
the no meagre sum of thirty-two dollars of as good
money as the country afforded, and as a present for
good behavior one hundred and twelve pounds dried
cod, besides giving me an air of independence I had
never before fully appreciated, which no doubt, boy-
like, was exhibited to the best advantage, especially
when entertaining ready listeners with the remarkable
incidents and hair-breadth escapes consequent to a
life on the ocean wave:

> Where the blue waters leap,
> While our watch we keep,
> And the gallant old ship
> Ploughs he furrows so deep.

CHAPTER VI.

SECOND VOYAGE TO THE STRAITS.

IN the balmy month of May, the Spring following, I shipped, on board the fore-topsail Schooner Franklin, of ninety tons burthen Capt Timothy Daggett commanding. As was the usual custom, the vessel was taken to Boston for her outfit, her crew of eleven men accompanying her, and on the tenth of the month cleared for another cruise to the Straits, Wanting masts, spreets &c., for our boats, and fuel for cooking purposes, after a good run put into Bay of Islands for a supply; thence to Shallow Bay, eighty miles, in a northeast course where we cast anchor. Here we fell in with Schooner Resolution, of Derby, Connecticut, under the command of James Stewart, who also was from the Vineyard. The crews of both vessels went on shore, and in the course of our rambles over this uninhabited part, of creation we suddenly came upon a newly-made grave. Some curiosity was manifested and no little fear was traceable on the countenances of our companions, as one proceeded to read the inscription attached to the headboard, which revealed the fact that the occupant of this lonely burial place was a victim to the uncurbed wrath of a mulatto who had been living with this individual and his brother, while spending the season just past, for the purpose of hunting moose, fox and other game, of which there was an abundance. We afterward learned that the murderer was caught and, contrary to the present manner of disposing of such unmitigated criminals, was dealt with according to the justice of a death sentence.

As total abstinence was not in those days a prevailing virtue, it was not strange that among the crews of these vessels were to be found men, who sometimes indulged with no slight degree of freedom in those beverages so well calculated to destroy their usefulness, filching from them every high and· noble aspiration which the Creator intended for a more elevating purpose than the simple gratification of an appetite, productive of results alike fatal to ones-self and to those with whom he comes in contact. While on shore, the " Little Brown Jug " (doubtless a near relative to that alluded to in the popular song of that name), was often consulted, its contents imparting to the men a slightly elevated sensation, which enabled them to see things in a very different light than they really existed. Thus we readily account for a fright quite a number of our men experienced, and which came near terminating in a tragical manner. One of the crew (in after life familiarly known as Uncle Lot), who, unlike his namesake of ancient days, was possessed of a companion who was never known to look back, but with him met the struggle of life with an unyielding decision and determination ; while for many years of their declining life their lamps were trimmed and burning, guiding the tempest-tossed mariner in safety to a desired haven, as gladly to the sailor's gaze, Cape Pogue lighthouse sends its glimmering beams over the waters of Vineyard Sound.

But returning to "the thread of our discourse," as a good brother sometimes expresses himself. Uncle Lot going in land in advance of his companions, being rather of a fun-loving disposition, fully in the belief that " a good joke now and then is relished by the best of men," and therefore not a criminal offence, thought he would try what effect a little one might have. Secreting himself behind some vines and bushes near a number of trees, which he judged his shipmates would soon attempt to cut down, divesting himself of his coat, pants and hat, bringing his red flannel shirt and drawers in view and drawing over his face and head a bright crimson bandanna, he lay perfectly quiet awaiting the approach of his victims. Presently advancing footsteps were heard, and it was not long before the work of chopping began, a portion of the men only waiting as lookers-on, intending to assist in conveying the wood to the boats when it was in readiness. Suddenly rising from his ambush and shouting in imitation of the wild Indian whoop, he startled them most fearfully. Quickly gathering (not the wood), but their remaining strength for a stampede, they cried aloud " Red Indians! red Indians! help! help! and made for the shore, one of the party covering his retreat with a heavily loaded shot-gun, of which, in case the supposed foe had been found to be gaining on him, he would not have hesitated in lending him the contents. The boats gained, no time was lost in regaining the vessel, where they were assisted on board so pale and terrified, there nearest relations would hardly have recognized them. At the dinner-table the story was related, and when at last the cause of so much trouble was found to be a little joke of Uncle Lot's, a hearty laugh went round and good cheer was contagious.

The night following the day so propitious "for the race" was very calm; the vessels lay within a cable's length of each other, which, as it was dead low water, brought us very near the shore. By and by the silence which reigned around was disturbed, as the rattling of stones on shore and the apparent moving of the hulk of an old boat seemed to indicate something approaching, which readily suggested to our already excited imaginations the certainty that the Indians were about to attack us. Fully armed to repel boarders, anxiously we awaited their arrival until the day dawned; when hastily our anchors were taken, and with our boats we towed out to sea, preferring to trust ourselves to the mercy of the ocean than to fall into the clutches of a merciless foe. We afterwards felt somewhat chagrined to learn that our fears were entirely groundless, being caused simply by the scratching of birds, industriously seeking crabs and other nutriment on which they subsisted, only being able to procure them when the tide was out. We went on our way rejoicing Arriving after a three days passage at Brador Gulch, where fishing commenced, and we procured two-thirds of a fare, the fish striking to the Eastward soon after. We followed on to Red Bay and completed the voyage, having a favorable passage of ten days, curing our fish in part, at or near where now reaches out in the waters of Katama Bay, the favorite landing for the thousands who come to enjoy its quiet scenes, and reap the benefit of the refreshing seaside facilities so abundantly afforded. So terminates another voyage at sea, for which I was paid off at the rate of ten dollars per month, thus enabling me to give to my dear old mother forty dollars as a little present, which was very acceptable, for I, being the eldest of the children, it was but little the others could do, and every item that I was competant to add to the treasury was carefully and judiciously invested. With feelings of mingled pride and gratitude does memory of the past (associated with the warm affection and reverential awe which I ever felt for my pa-

rents) even now, when trembling limbs and silver locks
remind me that the voyage of life will soon be over,
gild the horizon of my declining sun with the hope of
at last gaining a safe anchorage.

> " Near that blessed shore
> Where tempests ne'er break
> Or billows roar."

CHAPTER VII.

AKING a short stay on shore, joined the sloop Elinor, of Troy, N. Y., freighting flour and grain from Troy and Albany to Boston, continued in the same employment on board this craft for three seasons. Late in the Fall, after putting the vessel in good condition for the rough coasting in the inclement weather of an aproaching Winter, was loaded at New York with a cargo of flour, cheese, and dead hogs, for the Boston market. At one o'clock P. M. we left port. A strong westerly wind, or rather gale it might better be called, brought us down L. I. Sound a humming, though able to carry but little sail. It getting to be nearly dark, we judged the course steared would clear Block Island, but the mainsail being on the port side, our craft stole to windward of her course, and before we had time to haul off shore after making the discovery, to our horror fetched up on the rocks bounding the north west point of Block Island. Immediately jibbing the mainsail and giving her a part of the jib,

37

she forged over, and before the main sheet could be
hauled aft struck hard and fast on the bar inside the
point, thumping heavily, she soon bilged and began
to break up. It was very rough, the sea making a
clean breach over us, but the boom being in shore
heeled her that way, making it possible for us to
save ourselves, which at first looked rather dubious.
Bitter cold, as it was, our boats riddled the dead-lights
broken in, and the cabin fast filling with water, our
escape from an ocean grave would seem almost a
miracle. Until daylight approached we stood in the
water. Then warned by our bottomless wreck that
what we were to do to save ourselves must be done
speedily, we crawled upon deck to take a survey, and
discovered a man upon the beach who informed us,
that as it was now low water, we must effect a landing immediately or not at all. Our complement of
men consisted of five, each of whom was considering
the surest way to extricate himself from the threatening danger. The ground froze as fast as the water
receded, and you may judge how soft was the landing,
as we swung from the weather rail toward the shore,
by the jib halliards, letting go our hold when over-
reaching the water, fifteen or twenty feet in the air.
In this manner we all succeeded in landing safely,
with the exception of several severe bruises, which
were constant reminders of that unfortunate cruise for
many long days and nights after. But getting from

the wreck was not destined to end our grief or con-
summate our troubles. Observing some mile and a half
inland a residence, we started for it, but soon came
to a pond frozen over, which we preferred to cross
rather than go around, as the incessant cold was fast
benumbing us. Had proceeded to near the middle
of it, when it began to crack, and finally let us in altogether. As fast as the circumstances of the case
would permit, we fought our way to the shore nearest
the house, upon reaching which, its hospitable doors
were opened and a cordial invitation was extended to
enter. We were not slow in accepting. A cheerful
fire and warm drink soon made us quite comfortable,
and before many hours " Richard was himself again."
After a good night's rest we repared to the beach, and
succeeded in saving a few articles of our personal
effects, as well as small quantities of the freight.
With the spars and sails, the latter was sold, and to
the families who had so generously entertained us we
gave the hull of the craft.

The severe weather detained us upon the island for
three weeks, when we were taken away by a little
Pilot Boat bound to and belonging in Holmes Hole.
We anticipated a short run down the Sound, but when
only half the distance to Gay Head had been accomplished, a strong gale arising, were compelled to scud
for a lee port, which we made at Stonington, waiting
one week for a favorable opportunity. Got home all

right at last. As freighting was now quite dull on
account of the embargo, and wages consequently low,
I thought best to remain ashore, which I did, working
a little here and there until the Winter wore away.
When Spring opened, the herring fishery of our own
island affording something better than idleness, I turned
my attention to that interest. And, by the way, I
will try to give you a slight description of this ancient
enterprise, and moreover tell you how it has come to
pass that the Old Mattakusett has "gone up."

CHAPTER VIII.

IKE most of the inlets, ponds, coves and villages, the fishery alluded to, bears an Indian cognomen, and without doubt Mr. Indian had an interest in the so-called Mattakeesett Creek previous to the settlement of the island by the whites. At any rate, the oldest inhabitant cannot remember when its running waters did not invite the finny tribe to its precincts, though it has long since changed almost for its entire length. Running parallel with the south beach for a gon distance, the surge of the broad Atlantic con--lstantly narrowing the space between shore and creek it has been filled up many times, and re-dug further north-east, until any traces of the old Indian property would be difficult to find. For many years afterward it was considered personal property, and whosoever owned a share therein was considered a fortunate man, for in it he saw something strongly resembling the " Widow's Cruise," of oil, which could not fail. Happy, indeed, was the individual who owned " two-

41

sixths," for that was almost a competency, especially if the season was a fortunate one.

Fishing in this creek, was, early in its history, reduced to a system by the fathers, from which the sons have never materially departed. The ownership of the property once fully established, it was sufficiently secured against any encroachments, and in just proportions was dealt out each person's share of the catch, after necessary expenses attending the same were deducted. The whole interest was divided into quarters, each quarter bearing a name by which it was always recognized, viz.; Jenkin's, Plain, Town, and Chappaquidic; each using twenty-four hours as they came, respectively. Each quarter was divided and sub-divided, even to sixty-fourths, thereby giving to the owners of a sixty-fourth, one fish out of every sixty-four taken; and so proportionately those representing a larger share. Each full share, (that is, every sixth,) was supposed to provide a man to represent it. Others appearing and tendering their services, were termed " Reformators." Why such a name was thus applied has always remained a secret, unless it was that persons who were accustomed to mingle there having become somewhat demoralized, it was thought best to give them the benefit of outside influence. Be it so or not, they were usually compensated, (prior to the division being made,) by the Agent, in council with the proprietors, deciding how many herring were justly due. The number being named, they were instructed to do their own counting; and frequently being very poor at figures, the bag was filled without regard to accuracy; requiring two or three men to handle it, when, if no error existed in the count, a small boy could easily have shouldered it. But such is life; we have had Reformators in every age.

Six nets were generally used in catching, three on each side of the creek, between which boards placed edgeways divided the passage of the waters in the middle. At the weirs, the creek was some seven or eight feet wide. Near by, on the bank, were large boxes, capable of containing sixty barrels of fish each, which sometimes had to be emptied to make room for those taken later. They were removed from the boxes, or "kids" as they are denominated by the fishermen, in half-barrel strap tubs and credited to the different shares, the account of which was chalked down on the tail-board of somebody's cart, usually by the agent of the Quarter. Opposite the net-handles were small houses which in bad weather were very convenient. These were designated "Ballicators." Here, too, I am in the dark for an explanation, after swallowing "Webster on a bridge." If any of you should at any future period make a dictionary, you will confer a great favor by defining in it the word "Ballicator." The houses resembled, and were quite suggestive of, sentry boxes as seen upon a fort, capable of seating one man and affording a shelter from wind and rain.

It was not an uncommon thing for disputes to arise in regard to the division of the fish, and not unfrequently the disputants would engage in a fist fight, until one or more would (accidently of course) be tumbled into the water, thereby getting cooled off, when business would be resumed. The first catch of the season began as early as March, continuing until June whenthe fish that had escaped the vigilance of the fisher men, or had been allowed to pass unmolested between sunset of Saturday night and the same hour of Sunday, having deposited their spawn in the fresh ponds above, came down on their passage to the sea. Often thirty or even forty men and boys might be seen in and around the creek-house, ready to do whatever offered in catching, dividing, &c, sometimes securing from three to four hundred barrels in twenty-four hours, at which time these men would leave, giving room for the next party to commence operations. When so many fish were taken, it was attended with a degree of excitement which at times was quite animating; and this fishery being the most celebrated artifical one in the country, it often attracted visitors from abroad, — ladies as well as gentlemen. Moreover, the road leading thereto, across the Great Plains, furnished a most desirable ride in pleasant weather, giving to strangers an opportunity (which they appeared fully to appreciate) of walking on the surf-bound shores of the Atlantic, beholding its beauty, and majesty as mountains high it rolled its gigantic waves far up the beach.

When, as frequently was the case, the fish showed no disposition to run up, in latter years (more especially) long sticks were used in driving them, requiring considerable skill to do it successfully. At these times there was a *King*, who, with his long booted subjects, would quietly go to where the creek emptied into the salt-water, and when any considerable number entered a rush was made, and their retreat was cut off, by placing very deep nets across the creek. Then the pounding and splashing would finally persuade the fish to go up, rather than have the life pelted out of them. Sometimes getting very thick together, the fish, (apparently in a flurry), would all with one accord make a bee line for the nets above, raising the water in advance of them, all foaming nearly a foot high. Now, for a time, the sight is novel, indeed. Perhaps in less time than it requires to describe it, twenty or thirty barrels are secured. The habits of the fish are very regular. They will not enter the creek only at particular times, not even obeying the mandates of the King, who has probably had to do with more herring than any other man in the whole country, he having given them some awful smokings. When the fish do not appear there is but little work done. Then it is that the evil one finds any quantity of mischief for idle hands to do.

The house alluded to was roughly furnished with

berths of hard pine, also long plank seats, both of
which were used by the sleepy ones to stretch out
upon, when the floor was not preferred or considered
most safe, as sometimes accidents happen in the house
as well as in the open air.   As it frequently proved,
sleeping was not an indulgence much courted by the
denizens of this favorite resort.   The uninitiated, however, overcome by weariness, almost unconsciously,
would sometimes find a little nap disturbed by the loud
shouts and boisterous laughter of a jolly crowd, who
very innocently were gazing on a countenance well
begrimed with lamp-black.   At another time some victim would be aroused from the land of bright dreams,
feeling a disagreeable sensation of suffocation, caused
by the chimney-top being filled with hay or other
stuffing, preventing the natural escape of smoke from
the fire-place below.   At such times the individual
victimized would make a dash for the door, only to be
confronted by some hideous or ghostly figure, or perhaps to fall headlong into the half-hogshead of slime
and water, so disposed that to shun it was impossible.
Occasionally one might find himself elevated, or sus-
pended by his heels to the rafters or beam girting the
building.   When a general wakefulness prevailed, the
weary hours of night were beguiled by story-telling
and song-singing, though maybe not of the most refined character.

The bay into which the creek emptied was a favor-

able place for striped-bass-catching, which was to some
extent practised by those who frequented the herring
fishery, by baiting a hook with part of a fish, thrown
far off from the shore, it was allowed to remain until
the fish in search of food, would greedily attempt to
swallow it, when he would get hooked so securely
that he would soon die. The owner of the line looked
to it occasionally through the night. Not unfreqnently,
however, the pleasant anticipation of the fisherman
would vanish after a hard and long pull, discovering
(not a large bass, as he fancied,) but maybe an over-
grown sheep which some lover of fun had procured
from a neighboring farm, and attached to the line in
the temporary absence of the proprietor. Such was
the place where many days and nights of my life
were passed,—usually receiving good pay, sometimes
in fish, at other times cash. This fishery was a source
of no inconsiderable income to the inhabitants of the
island generally. Most any business interest could
easily determine when it was in a flourishing condition, by the influx of money, which, readily changing
hands, made trade lively, giving to the place a healthy
spirit of activity.

Fences in that immediate vicinity were not allowed
to remain more than one season, for almost of a certainty some cold dark night would they be used for
firewood.

A few years ago, the creek being in a somewhat

dilapidated condition, almost the whole interest being represented by the *King* and a few faithful followers, who cared more, seemingly, to catch every fish who dared to invade its waters, rather than to make any improvements, a number of very wicked men conceived the idea of letting the salt water into the nursery above, by tapping the beach which divided it from the ocean. For a long time guards were stationed at the various localities most propitious for so vile a purpose, to prevent, if possible, such a disaster. But finally the vigi_ lance of the guards becoming bankrupt, digging began, and before daylight betrayed the "Diggers," (as they were termed,) a ship channel was made and the pond so reduced that the creek became useless. The main object in opening the beach was : that passing shoals of herring and other members of the finny family might have a suitable port of entry, where in large quantities they might be taken by the illegal process of seining. The parties supposed to be engaged in so nefarious a work, were placed under arrest, tried and permitted to give bail for further examination, which resulted in their acquittal, their case being argued by Hon. B. F. Butler, a lawyer of some eminence, and for a number of years a member of Congress. He from the fact (possibly) of his being slightly crosseyed, was unable to see that the rights of Mattakeesett had been invaded ; representing with no little show of truthfulness, that no such fishery in fact existed, as the spot originally granted was half a mile out to sea.

And now, having given you quite an elaborate history of an interest which for a century supplied the markets of New England and the South-west with a great table luxury, besides attracting to our shores fish of larger species, which was not only desirable, but exceedingly profitable, asking your pardon for a seeming digression, I will continue my narrative, which brings me to the nineteenth year of my age, when I joined the little Pilot-boat, Exchange, for a season of fishing on the shoals south of Nantucket.

CHAPTER IX.

OUR vessel was under the command of a Captain Dunham, with a crew of five men and her cook, in which latter capacity I served, with the understanding that for the services rendered I was to receive all the fish caught by myself, — which proved a good arangement on my part, as my line stood "high hook." The reason why may be easily explained, it being partially from industrious habits, but more particularly perhaps from strict adherance to temperance principles, which I am sorry to say was rather the exception than the general rule in practice on board our vessel, many a good opportunity sliding by while our men were sleeping off the ill effects of their boozy carousals. After being out nearly a week, it was thought best to make a harbor, as the jugs were about drained, and they could not stand the pressure of their departed spirit's with any degree of· comfort or composure. So the craft was headed for Chatham, and notwithstanding it was blowing a gale heedless of consequences, in such haste were they to gain the land that a fresh supply might be procured, sail was crowded on to such a degree that the mainmast was badly sprung, besides very nearly numbering our mess as each moment, wave after wave threatend to engulf us. Good luck rather than skillful management, at nightfall of a Saturday, enabled us to reach port. Without delay a messenger was dispatched for the article in question, which already on that, as on many other occassions, had so nearly proved the destroyer of both body and soul of men illy prepared to meet such a fearful end. The following morning opened finely, our captain in his suit of go-on-shore apparel told me of his intention to attend church, wished me to set him on shore and watch for his return to take him on board again, and be sure not to keep him long in waiting. The crew preferring to remain with the vessel, did so, spending the day in the gratification of an appetite which seemed to control and master all the better feelings and emotions of their nature. This they took pleasure in demonstrating in various methods, one of which proving very nearly fatal to myself, I will speak of.

When the hour had about arrived for the Captain to return, some of the crew, thinking to embarrass my ability to obey his order, filled the boat with water, then in a commanding voice told me to jump in and bail her out. At first, feeling somewhat angry, I flatly refused; whereupon I was told if the order was not

immediately complied with, they would throw me into
the ocean. Still refusing, they made good their word,
and roughly clutching me when a little off my guard,
regardless of my cries that I could not swim, tumbled
me headlong over the vessel's side. One, more human
than his companions, seeing my fruitless endeavors to
regain the vessel, threw over a rope, by the aid of
which I succeeded in crawling in the water-logged
boat. Receiving a bucket, I lost no time in clearing
the boat from the water, as I was assured the experience already received was but a preliminary to what
might be expected if further refusal was persisted in.
Soon the voice of the captain warned me of his approach, and as speedily as possible I finished bailing
and pulled in after him. Somewhat displeased that he
was kept waiting, he inquired the cause, and when
informed that others were more to blame than myself,
he swore roundly, threatening to reduce each man's
allowance fo rum to three quarts per day.

Soon got under way and in a few hours were on
good fishing ground. Remained this time two or three
weeks, when a fearful gale from the eastward caused
us to make for a port. Not a stich of canvas could
be carried, and under bare poles we scud like the
wind, the fury of which we were endeavoring to es-.
cape. It was dark when we entered Edgartown harbor, ran in under Tower Hill, let go both anchors,
which they dragged, and high and dry up the beach we

went. By removing a part of the fish we shortly hove her off, and went out on another trip, continuing them with varied success and unimportant incidents until the closing of the season.

During the Fall and Winter of 1803 passed my time much as I had in previous Winters, when not on shipboard, endeavoring to earn an honest penny, sometime claming and eeling or clearing woodland (" stumping," as . it was called, though not exactly in the sense it is generally understood at the present day); but procuring the means of smoothing, to the best of my abilities, the pathway fo my still surviving parent and the family looking to us for support. Early in April of the same year, on board the sloop-smack Democrat, C. Pease, followed fishing on the south side of Nantucket, marketing our fares at New Bedford. Afterward, as the season became more favorable, we changed our business for the lobster trade, where along the shores of Cape Cod we would make up our load, disposing of it to New York dealers. Five or six weeks were usually consumed in making a round trip. On one of these trips we were run down by a large schooner bound in a different direction. It was dark at the time, and nothing was observed until the vessels collided. Our mainsail was badly torn, and the hull of our vessel amidships cut down, so that it appeared we could not long prevent sinking. However, by stuffing the open seams with old clothing, bags &c., we finally reached

port, repaired damages and resumed our trips, continuing them till fall. I then took to the woods again,
where felling trees and stubbing kept me engaged until
the North River sloop Eastern Trader offered me achance,
at twenty-two dollars per month. Our business was
freighting grain from Albany and New York to Boston. In order that you may have some idea of the
perils of weathering Cape Cod in the Winter season,
I will devote a few minutes, if agreeable, to the consideration of the subject.

CHAPTER X.

THE vessel was under the command of Captain Ripley, my former guardian, and here it may be well to mention that she was very low-decked, and consequently when laden the water would often flow over it, which in freezing weather did not have a tendency to increase the comfort of those on board. Soon after sun-rise, the tide serving right, we left the harbor of Edgartown, in company with a number of square riggers, and a top-sail sloop. A favorable wind took us down as far as the highlands of Cape Cod, when it changed into the north-west and blew a hurricane, and it became necessary to put the vessel under as snug sail as possible. This the extreme cold made very difficult to perform, especially as the clew of our mainsail was carried away, and in lowering down we could not well avoid dropping it into the water. As we got it on board it immediately stiffened with ice, but at last we got in three reefs, and with a tackle on boom-end hooked on to the flue, hauled out as well as we could and reset it. Took bonnet off the jib and

55

stood off· shore, making .a north-east course ; ran till
morning and then wore ship standing in to the westward, the hull of our vessel looking like a floating
iceberg, being fairly logged with the quantity of ice
that had collected, almost hiding our identity. We
fetched in as near Chatham beach as the wind allowed,
let go the anchor, and set colors in the rigging
" union down," for assistance, which very soon attracted the attention of a number of men who came to
our relief. Our captain asked if they could get us in,
which, after clearing the craft of her formidable load,
they succeeded in doing, to our great joy. In order
to avoid large quantities of drifting ice which came
down with the ebb tide, while we had one anchor in
the channel, another was taken on to the shore, which
hauled us close in out of a strong current, as we just
kept the channel cable tight, without fear of grounding, and at flood tide swung by it.

The tops'l sloop with one schooner, soon after came
in ; also a brig, which had been run down, during the
night, dropped her anchor a little to the leeward of us
in a crippled condition. The vessel with which she
had been in contact doubtless sank, and her unfortunate crew found a watery grave. Thus, from a fleet
of over forty sail only four succeeded in making an
anchorage, the others being driven out to sea.

Learning the particulars of the sad catastrophe to
which I have alluded, we found that the first blow re-

ceived by the brig carried the bowsprit by the board close up to the stem, and broke the anchor flue. She next got a blow 'midships, which cut her down till the cotton in the hold and on deck fetched her up. By this time the water was running in, but by opening the bales of cotton and stuffing the gaps, she was kept afloat, and by lashing the kedge-anchor to the broken flue and letting go, they were enabled to outride the gale. We lay there a number of days. Our provisions giving out, went ashore and bought what we could ; we also butchered a bullock which was divided among the several crews. Thus making the best of a bad bargain, finally one Sunday morning the weather moderating, it looked favorable for a start. The mate was ashore, which somewhat delayed us, but we took the shore anchor in, letting the vessel swing into the channel, and anxiously waited for the mate. Presently a large field of ice came sweeping down with a strong tide, which piled in upon us, running up the rigging a dozen feet high, then falling with a crash upon deck. Directly our cable parted, and unable to help ourselves, we were crowded upon a shoal, broadside to the ice, which threatened to demolish us. About this time the mate arrived and as the tide gradually slacked, cleared the ice, and by a small anchor hove off and returned to our former anchorage, but with the loss of our large anchor. We hired the longshoremen to try and recover it for us, but they not exerting themselves much, it was lost to us, Doubtless when they were disposed to attend to the matter it was not much of a job; it probably paid better to get it for themselves than to have secured it for us.

We left in a few days in company with the topsail sloop, and got into Boston Bay, taking another snow-storm and easterly gale. The sloop was just on our weather bow, heading as nearly as possible for Boston light, when a heavy sea boarded her, breaking the stern boat clear from her beyond recovery. Not long after, glad enough and tired enough, we tied up at Long Wharf, and the sloop near by at Central. Both vessels soon had good fires going, to warm their crews and dry their clothing. Directly the alarm of fire was sounded, and hastening on deck we found that on board the sloop too much of a good thing was proving injurious. The wooden funnel leading from the old-fashioned fire-place, (commonly used in those days) having taken fire and communicated to the spars and sails, needed attention, which it soon received and the flames were extinguished, with only the loss of ·articles mentioned. Our cargo was sold in lots to suit customers. We then made other cruises to the west and returning, not always having so rough a time, but generally requiring about three weeks to go and return. This business I continued until late in the Fall, when the vessel went into Winter quarters, resuming it again in the Spring.

CHAPTER XI.

CONSIDERING myself by this time old enough to appreciate female society, it may not appear strange that my thoughts sometimes roamed o'er the broad domain of fancy, in quest of an object on which to place my affections, as I pictured in my imagination a little home of my own, which I hoped in the future to share with somebody's daughter. About this time a circumstance did occur, though slight in itself, which in its final results had the effect of changing the whole tenor of my life ; and many times since, when congratulating myself on the good fortune attending me, I have been led to say,— it was the only genuine streak of good luck I ever did have.

The trouble between our Country and Great Britain having been settled, commerce revived and business interests on sea and land generally improved. Yet awaiting an opportunity just suiting my wishes, I remained ashore, or occasionally made short cruises in and about the fishing waters of Vineyard Sound or out

the south side of the island, for a sword-fish expedition or a cod-fish voyage, usually returning quite
early in the day. Upon my return from one of these
excursions, having carelessly neglected taking along
my rations, the gnawings of hunger hastened my footsteps to the home of my mother and the little family,
who, upon arriving, I found to be out making calls.
Not .being a stranger to the cupboard, I soon refreshed
myself and sat down to meditate. I was soon in a
brown study, and the autumnal sun went down e'er
my revery was disturbed. But shortly after, the voice
of the lady who occupied the lower tenement, (Mrs.
Pent) aroused me, as from the foot of the stairs she
informed me of the presence of two young ladies
whose acquaintance she wished me to form, adding
that I must change my clothes as soon as possible and
present myself. Not being the possessor of so elaborate a wardrobe as is considered necessary at the present day, I was not long in deciding what I should
adopt. Soon attired, I "reported for duty" by entering the presence of the company, to whom I was introduced and endeavored to make as good an impression as possible. Have since ound out that they never
would have mistrusted that I was half as green as I
fancied myself. Their call was not a long one, and,
if I remember correctly there was not much that I
found to talk about: which possibly will account for
my not being taken for a verdant youth. But the

real fact in the matter is, that as often as I cast my eyes toward the particular location occupied by one, it became almost impossible to utter a sentence, and from that brief interview the discovery was made that the heart so long all my own (as regards matrimonial inclinations) had been captivated by one I had never before met. After the ladies left the house, Mrs. Pent (or, as better known later in life, "Aunt Debby," from the uniform kindness of heart and christian spirit she ever manifested) asked me what I thought of the girls. My reply was that they appeared very pleasant. Being still further interrogated, confessed my preference for Miss Stewart, adding the assurance that if she would not refuse me, I would marry her as I was a living man. " O," says Aunt Derby, " you are joking." My reply was, " You wait and see ; for as I am a living Jethro, she shall be my wife if I can get her. Which promise, I am proud to say, was kept five years afterward, to the joy and comfort of a long and check-ered life.

CHAPTER XII.

THE young lady to whom I have alluded was the daughter of a well-to-do farmer, who, possessing no ordinary talents in the art of husbandry, was amply rewarded, as his successful improvements in agricultural implements and abundant harvests indicated. If advice was needed or suggestions were to be made, Farmer Benjamin Stewart must be consulted, and his views and opinions received as decisive. The family consisted of two sons and one daughter beside her already referred to, each in some degree inheriting the proud spirit and noble ambition of the father. With the exception of the eldest son, they all appeared to take delight in the honorable calling of agriculture. He, early in life, manifested a* strong desire to follow the sea, thinking a farmer's life too tame to suit his roving propensities. Starting when but a lad, he made a number of voyages in the whaling business, till returning from one he was captured by

62 .

an English Man-of-war, and all hands made prisoners, some of them being sent to England, the remainder, including himself, being held on board the war ship. They destroyed the whaler, which was the Mary Ann, belonging to the island of Nantucket. Here it was that the vim of the family was clearly demonstrated, and the stubborn will of Sam, the son of Benjamin, Britian's heel could not subdue.

Nearing our coast, it was remarked by the Admiral that getting short of provisions, they must put in somewhere for a supply. Overhearing the talk, our ex-whaleman replied, " Sir, I can tell you where you may be supplied." Said he, " can you take us in where our stores can be recruited?" " I can, sir ; New York is a grand place, I will take you right in." "For your impudence," he replied, "you will form the acquaintance of Dartmoor Prison." And it was not long before his words were verified.

While on board the ship he flatly refused to touch his hat to the British officers, which greatly aggravated them ; but no punishment that was threatened induced him to comply, which oftentimes cost him severe treatment. Such was the determined spirit of one of the family, which to a greater or less degree was apparent in the character of each of the others, not excepting my intended. But to dispose of Sam, whom I have taken the liberty to introduce to you, permit me to add that after a long confinement in the filthy dungeon, he was liberated in order to take command of the English ship Elizabeth, bound on a whaling cruise. The ship was taken by the natives, during the voyage, but subsequently was recaptured through the daring bravery of her Captain, and safely returned with a valuable cargo of oil. He made a number of voy ages, which proving successful, placed him in comfort able circumstances, which he made more so by taking to his heart and home a most amiable and lovely English lady for whom he had formed an attachment.

A few years after he was supposed to have been poisoned by the natives, whom he visted while still pursuing his favorite calling. A few years since, one of his sons came to America and visited the childhoods home of his departed parent. What his opinion of the premises was we are unable to conjecture ; but if fond of a quiet life and the constant roll of the ocean, he could not have failed to enjoy the scene to his heart's content.

Fresh in our memory are the scenes of our childhood,
Forget them we'll never by night or by day ;
Old ocean and plain, the scrub-oak and wildwood.
Make familar the spot where in youth we did play.

CHAPTER XIII.

ALMOST A HERO.

efore I continue this yarn any farther, I must tell you an old story, an incident which occurred during the turbulent days in the latter part of the war of 1812, which came near making a hero of your humble servant.

"There is a destiny that shapes our ends, .
Rough hew them as we will."

Early in the morning of a very fine day, a number of men strolling on the south beach of Martha's Vineyard, discovered among the reefs a vessel displaying signals for a pilot. Immediately shoving off a small boat kept for that purpose, they boarded her and found her to be a prize to an English Convoy, that had recently been prowling around in company with a Man-of-war. The vessel captured was just returning with a load of cod-fish, and her crew was prisoners in the hold of the vessel which had been partially emptied of fish for their reception The officer in command requested to be taken into some neutral port for sup plies. Accordingly she was cleared from the shoals, and after a few hours anchored between the lighthouse in Edgatown harbor and Chappaquiddic point opposite. Observing her and judging that one of our fishing fleet had arrived, with a neighbor I launched a skiff and pulled off to have a "gam," not apprehending the least danger until to late to retreat. Ran alongside, and, our warp being passed, we were invited by the officer of the deck to come on board, discovering to our dismay that instead of her being what we supposed, she belonged to Her Majesty's service. But putting on the best face possible, I replied to the questions put by the commander as if we perfectly understood our position.

Said he to me, " Are you aware what kind of a craft you have visited?" In reply, very indifferently I assured him that I did know. For I had observed previously to gaining the deck, that the buttons on his coat bore the emblems of the English Navy, insteadof those representing our own. Trying what effect his words might have upon us, we were told that we would not be allowed to leave the vessel ; to which in reply, I said "I think, sir, you will be gentlemanly enough,. when we are disposed to leave (which we are in no hurry to do), to permit us to do so." "Yes, O yes ; certainly ; I was only joking " "But," he continued,'' we are out of small stores, and you must furnish · us with what are needed without any money, aswe have none to pay." I told him it was not in accordance with my feelings to feed my enemies. "But," said he, "does not your Bible teach you so to do?" "Well, at any rate, you cannot expect to be furnished with provisions without remuneration. 'Ah,' said he, "I have it now! In our vessel's hold is stowed a quantity of dried fish, in exchange for which you must satisfy our demand." This we agreed to do, and preparation being made to take our leave, he communicated the countersign, which was supposed to insure attention from the night sentry, at which time he recommended us to return. On reaching shore, we immediately repared to a grocery near by, kept by one Thomas Mayhew, who very willingly supplied the requisition which in due time was conveyed to the vessel. On our near approach, as previously instructed, we rested on our oars, in order to attract the attention of the sentinel. He failing to appear, we ran alongside and gained the deck, where, upon looking around, we discovered to our amazement and surprise that we were masters of the position, the sentry not to be found, and the vessel's company asleep below decks! Proceeding forward, where the cabin in such craft usually was built, found the scuttle nearly closed, which fact I was not long in communicating to my companion, informing him that by shutting the slide and dropping into the clasp a thole pin, the anchor could be slipped, the vessel beached, and all her crew and officers would become prisoners to our little strategy. Said he, " It will never do," fearful that it coming to the ears of Her Majesty, our town would have to suf fer the consequences. Very reluctantly the idea was abandoned; making our presence known, such a tumbling up stairs was never before heard of. In such a hurry were they, a number came . near receiving fatal injuries by getting so completely wedged together, it was with difficulty that they were extricated.

The goods being received on board, the fish were passed into the boat in generous quantities, so many in fact, I feared the intention of the officers was to sink us; at last I begged them to desist, crying " enough ! enough !" when the order was given to " cease firing." We then rowed for the shore, the vessel soon after taking her departure of the pilot, who still remained on board, only leaving her when the foot of the shoals was reached, receiving, as we subsequently learned, twenty-five dollars in hard specie for the service he rendered. •

The fish thus received from our midnight excursion were sold for a good price, and the whole affair regarded as a profitable investment. Yet it was difficult to rid myself for years after, of the tormenting thought that I had lost, beyond the hope of recovery, the only opportunity ever offered to do a big thing. But as every thing happening is for the best, I accepted the consolation of this reflection, still persuing my humble walks in life.

CHAPTER XIV.

FIRST VOYAGE IN A SQUARE RIGGER.

SOON after peace was proclaimed, a small sloop came into our harbor for the purpose of procuring men who were willing to proceed to Portland, Me., to assist in bringing to Bristol, R. I., the ship Gen. Jackson, a five hundred ton prize to the privateer, Yankee, of Bristol. With a number of others I agreed o go for the sum of twenty dollars for the run. On arriving at the place designated, found that as the vessel was yet to be loaded, our services were required in getting the cargo on board, for which we received daily wages. Her hold was stowed off with a variety of small lumber, and on deck were taken spars and heavy timber.

We left port with a fair wind, but to enjoy it long was not in our line of luck. Soon changing to a gale, and a snow-storm accompanying it, we were obliged to send down top-gallant yards and masts, close-reef the lower sails, and try to make the best we could of a bad bargain, as it was impossible to get back. Hauled the ship on the port tack, keeping her so for three or four days, when the weather became better and we resumed our course.

Got along very well until a thick fog enveloped us and the wind canted to the southward, finally dying away to a calm with a strong current setting to the northward. Indications of the near approach to land, by a roaring sound borne to us through the dense darkness, led us to the conclusion that it would be wisdom to throw the deep sea lead; which being done, we found shoal water, and at every trial, it was becoming beautifully less. Cleared away both anchors, overhauled a range of cables, ready to let go at a moments warning. Judging ourselves to be in the vicinity of South Shoal (which probably was correct), a light breeze springing up, we shot out clear, our pilot taking a departure on the supposition.

The fog and southerly winds continued to prevail, and we saw nothing to relieve our anxiety for a number of days.

At last our soundings indicated that we were in Block Island channel, and Block Island bearing west, southerly, four miles distant, shaped our course for Newport. Soon after, having spoken a vessel just out from there, entered the river and soon arrived at Bristol, where we were paid off and allowed to return home.

Thus terminated my first voyage in a vessel "square rigged." For a week I remained at home, which visit was very agreeably spent, — how and where for the greater part, we will leave our friends to imagine. But as I was making preparation for a longer voyage than I had hitherto made, there was much to be looked after, and I rather judge that part was pretty well attended to.

CHAPTER XV.

N the first of June, 1815, in company with two of my townsmen, I engaged passage on board a Connecticut sloop bound for Boston, a Vineyard pilot accompanying us, as the captain was not familiar with the waters of Boston Bay. A heavy gale, with the most vivid lightnings and deep muttering thunders, overtook us, when, to add to our discomfort, the pilot was taken suddenly ill and compelled to leave the deck. The captain, as already stated, being a stranger in these parts became greatly alarmed for our safety; but on my assuring him that I could take the craft safely in, he very readily gave up the charge to me. The wind soon favoring us, it was not long e'er, safe and sound, we ran along side the wharf, and instead of my passage costing me eight dollars as per agreement he offered to pay for my services, which I refused to accept. .

Without loss of time, my companions and I visited the shipping, and an offer was soon accepted to join the ship Maria, of three hundred tons burthen, bound

72

to Charleston, S. C., for a cargo of cotton for Liverpool. After getting out, finding the ship very crank, not being sufficiently ballasted, we put away for the nearest port, which was Norfolk, Va., got what was required, and proceeded to Alexandria for freight. Took in three thousand five hundred and sixty-four barrels of flour, and cleared for Barcelona in Spain. It was now July, and we were very glad to exchange the hot weather of that clime for the cooler breezes of the ocean.

We were not long in finding out that a tyrant, instead of a gentleman, was in command of the vessel, for before we left the Potomac river, he seized up and flogged two of the crew Getting out to sea, the pilot was discharged, just as Cape Henry was receding from our view; but hardly had he bade us farewell, when all hands were ordered aft, arranged in line on the port side of the quarter-deck, and told to look over the vessel's side. Said the brute in command, "What do you see"? Our reply was, Blue Water. "Yes," replied he, "We are now on *blue water;* and it will be a word and a blow, and the blow will come first! Go forward!" Thinks I to myself, that is rather a strange arrangement, anyway, and as to that blow coming first, it is a prospect difficult to regard with any degree of complacency. Upon joining my shipmates in the forecastle, I found it was a system that heretofore had never come under their nautical experi-

ence, and was not calculated to impress men of any
spirit with any very ardent feelings of reverential awe,
or even passive respect. At four o'clock on the third
day out, the order to rig pumps was given. On trying
them, found her to be leaking badly, and continued
pumping all night without being able to free her. A
strong breeze right aft made it useless to attempt to
regain the port we had left, but, in order too ease the
vessel, sent down the top hamper and close-reefed the
lower sails. The pumps did not stop for eighteen days
and nights, the whole of the time being passed upon
deck by the crew, who, "spell and spell," kept the
vessel afloat, while without going below, the eating
and drinking and the little sleep indulged in from ex-
haustion took place on the booby hatch. As yet, the
captain, mate and stevedore had made no exertion in
this direction, but quite frequently endeavored to punish as much of the ardent as they well could We
concluded that the important business in which we
were then engaged should be more equally divided.
This we respectfully communicated, and informed the
Capt. that unless we were assisted the ship might
sink ; and with one accord ceased our labors. He then
asked if she sucked, or why did the pumps stop, and
whose spell it was. Our reply was, that the spells
were all out. The hint was taken, and speaking to
the stevedore, and mate, he told them he supposed we
wanted spelling, and addressing us, told us to keep

the pumps in motion or we should sink. To which we replied, " Let her sink ; we can afford to sell out as cheap as you can. They immediately turned on, You can judge, of our condition, when, by standing on deck we could see, with every motion of the vessel, her whole upper deck-frame open and shut, exposing seams wide enough to thrust the whole hand in. Fortunately, having on board a lot of tallow candles, the wicks were removed and the tallow mixed with ashes· from the cook's galley, making a cement which was crowded intothe cracks of the upper works, by a man slung over the vessel's side. This kept out much water in smooth weather, but as soon as it was any way rough, out it would come and our labor would soon drift far away in our wake.

After a prolonged and tedious passage, arriving at Lisbon, she was thoroughly corked and proceeded on her voyage to Barcelona. When Gibralter was on our lee quarter, and a fair wind was giving us a noble run, as we came near· an English Man-of-war a shot was fired to heave to. Not regarding the hint, it was not long before the firing was repeated, sending a shot under our bow which somewhat startled our commander, as he judged they meant business, and the order was given to haul aback. This being done and the sails clewed up, we were boarded by the ship's boats in command of an officer, who told us if we had not stopped the next shot would have riddled us. Our papers being found correct, permission was granted us to proceed. Fair winds and beautiful weather enabled us soon after to reach the offing, where, for thirty days, we lay in quarantine, being from a foreign country. The inhabitants getting hungry for our inviting cargo, took ashore nearly one quarter while below the city; each barrel receiving a quart of water upon it ere they dared to touch it. This they ignorantly imagined would secure them against the danger of infection.

Custom House officers were constantly on hand, and very movement was watched by them. Large boats, rowed by ten or more full grown Spaniards, were used for transporting our cargo to the city one and a half miles distant. To me some of their capers appeared very simple. In approaching the vessel, a line thrown to them was sure to be kicked overboard, unless first they had seen it thoroughly cleansed by being washed alongside. Our thirty days expiring, the ship was taken up to the harbor, or mole as it was called, which was formed by a break-water. Three boats, one on each bow, and one out ahead, well manned by robust natives, and the pilot, served to take the ship to her moorings, where, in a tier of seventy or eighty vessels of different kinds and nationalities, we discharged the remainder of our cargo.

The city is walled in, having but two passes. No one is allowed to come in the same gate they go out; sen-

tinels armed to the teeth guard each gateway. No
person is allowed to take out of the city over ten dollars at a time. At night all passing in or out is
prohibited. Judging from observation, strict honesty,
was not proverbial among them; even among those
placed on guard for the security of life and property,
a propensity for stealing from one another prevailed to a
great extent, while the avariciousness manifested was
almost paralel with a rumseller. A pistareen was sufficient to bribe a sentry on almost any occasion, which
our crew, who brought the proceeds of our sales on
board, often practiced. The buildings of the city are
beautiful, many rearing their richly polished walls
seven stories high, (but 'tis to be hoped that, unlike
Boston, their roofs are not á la Mansard); the material
used in the construction of these noble monuments of
architecture is a light colored granite. The streets of
the city were literally unfited for walking, by the ac-
cumulation of mud, and so narrow that one vehicle
could hardly pass another. It was very manifest, however, that there was much wealth, which in sad con-
trast with the squalid wretchedness also apparent, did
not argue well for the government by which they were
controlled.

Our cargo was discharged as speedily as possible.
In the meantime, a complete suit of new sails being
required, a man was sent on board to take the measure
of our spars; which being done, the sails were placed

in the hands of females who cut and made them in the
best shape and in an incredibly short time. Quite
frequently, when not engaged with ship duties, we visited the different places of note, among them various
scenes of amusement, seeing much that to us was entirely new and strange.

The stores were usually well-stocked with goods of
the finest texture, the productions of most every country, which would make one's mouth water to possess.

On sunday, (that of course being a gala day), our
ships company were desirous to see the sights. Accordingly half a day was given us for liberty; one
watch in the forenoon, the other in the afternoon, and
the captain furnished us spending money. In my
wanderings I observed, among the endless variety that
took my eye, two very nice silk shawls. Remembering
my sister and sweet-heart, I left my money in exchange
for them, investing some little in trifles for myself.
Goods here were very cheap, and I found that my investment could not have been nearly as favorably
made in other parts of the world. .

Soon after, as our flour was all disposed of, ballast-
ing the ship was in order, a trip to the island of Evica,
a few days sail to the southward, being contemplated.
We sailed the next Sunday morning, with a free sheet
wind, studding sails alow and aloft. It getting to be
breakfast time, I repared to the galley for a pot of

cocoa, our favorite beverage about that time. A shipmate, who went with me for a similar purpose, bailed
from the coppers his well-filled cup, boiling hot, just
as I was in the act of reaching for some. Passing his
out over my back. As I stooped to get it, a loose
rope dangling under his cup caught it, capsizing its
contests full upon my back! I thought all hands were
called,—and so they were. My comrades gathered
around and soon relieved me of my flannel shirt, taking
with it the skin from the whole surface of my back.
I didn't want any more cocoa that day. The captain,
standing by, saw the accident, falling afoul of the
careless fellow, beat him without mercy, while vainly
I cried for him to desist, as the fatal turnover was un-
intentional and the man no more to blame than myself. "I intend," said the captain, "to teach him to
have his eyes about him." To help the matter, the
captain brought from the cabin a cup of rum, with
which was mixed the coarsest of brown sugar, and
poured it over my lacerated body, nearly depriving me
of what little sense I had left. A good passage to the
island was favorable to me, and upon arriving was
furnished by a Spanish lady with a quantity of cotton
bats, which she told us should be laid on after being
saturated with sweet oil. For fourteen days and nights
I could only lie with my face downward. The weather
was extremely hot, and the flies so troublesome I was
almost driven to desperation, and I improved so slow-

ly it was six months before I went on duty. After the wounds were healed, the cotton stuck out all over my back; if put upon exhibition, I am quite unable to decide what kind of a bird I should have been taken for. But 'to me, it bore a striking resemblance to a cotton plantation, of which I was sole proprietor.

During the day, our sand ballast was deliberately discharged by boating it ashore; but when darkness shielded us from observation, the shovels flew lively in throwing it over the side, — a thing strictly prohibited by harbor regulations. Soon the work of re-loading began. Our cargo was brought to us in lighters, and consisted in part of one hundred tons of salt, forty or fifty cords of cork in sheets as large as a good sized door, a quantity of wines, brandies, sweet oil, almonds figs, raisins, filberts, grapes and olives, also a lot of door-mats, brooms and brushes, manufactured from the grass which grew very abundantly in some parts of the island. The casks of liquor, like the rest of our freight, were first landed between decks, and after wards stowed in their appropriate place. While engaged in stowing the lower hold, the person hooking on to the casks neglecting to chock the next one to that just lowered away, was the cause of no little trouble as well as loss. The vessel heeling a little, the cask between decks fetched away, and crashing down into the lower hold, stove two on which it fell. All hands jumped to the spot and succeeded in saving half a cask by heading it up. Night soon coming on it was left. A short time after, the mate discovering only a pair of feet and legs hanging outside of the broken cask, concluded there must be a head somewhere ; which, on further search, he found in close proximity to the spirits. He took him by the heels and assisted him into proper position, asking the man if he was not weaned. Told him he looked like too old an individual to be sucking, and if he didn't take more care of himself he would be drunk as the "Divil," (being a native of Nantucket, he was unable to say *Devil*), It was this sucker who was to take the first anchor watch for the night, and, as readily presumed, before he called the next man to release him he was pretty well smashed, from the effects of another pull at the wine cask. At daylight all hands were called, and as no morning watch appeared on deck, inquiries were made as to who stood that watch. It appeared no one was called. On search being made, Mr. Faithful Guardian of the night was found in the vicinity of the previous day's accident. He had the appearance of a man who had been in close confinement for a number of years, and looking on the surroundings in amazment. Being asked why the watch to relieve him was not called, he replied, "I intended to speak to him, but thinking a little wine for the stomach's sake, had better be procured first, went below, and for the life of me was unable to find my way up again. Have been looking around half the night for the stanchion to climb up by, but think some one has taken it away, or there never was one on this ship." It was three days before he got straightened out so he could walk a crack, which he practised, usually fetching up in the lee-scuppers. After that little spree he was a weaned child, never afterward evincing the least inclination to indulge. He was one of our very best men generous to a fault, and kindly disposed to every one with whom he came in contact. With my long experience of the ups and downs of life, I am firmly of the opinion that, nine times out of ten, the victim of in temperance is naturally of the same easy and generous disposition, of him of whom we have told the .wine story. But in this case of our captain there was a grand exception to a general rule, for to have found in his whole machinery a single redeeming quality, a microscope of the greatest power would have been required. He however agreed with us in one thing, which was, to get to sea as quickly as possible, and we very soon completed the cargo and started for home. With a fair wind, we got along nobly the earlier part of the passage. Our ship, running off before the wind, had a wonderful faculty for yawning about, sometimes shaking the studding sails first on one side than on the other; endeavoring, as we used to say, to turn round and examine her wake to see how straight she went.

One day, with a strong breeze and all sail on her, myself and one other at the wheel vainly doing our very best to keep her steady, while the captain stood by cursing us roundly, said he "D — n your infernal souls, let go the wheel; I will steer within half a point." We let go, but stood by ready to take hold again when required. He allowed her to sheer, shaking the studding sails on one side, when he said he had not got the run of her yet; directly he had her almost aback the other way, when a sea struck the rudder under the starboard run. The first we saw was the old man flying, but not waiting to see him land, we grabbed the wheel and in an instant got her all right. That was more than could be said of the skipper, who had learned the lesson that it was a soft thing to fly but extremly hard alighting. He gathered himself up, in a most indigant manner cursed the ship, the man who built her, her owners and the place where she was constructed. No more was said that day about bad steering or crooked wakes. Kicks and cuffs were the order, fore and aft, wherever his pious footsteps led him. Every man on board the ship received a flogging some time during the voyage, with the exception of a townsman of mine and myself. We had agreed, if any one escaped his chastening rod, as a forfeit to the crew, an oyster supper should be furnished. I endeavored to keep clear of the flogging to the best of my abilites, and succeeded; not that I feared being

killed or seriously injured, but did not fancy the name
of it. On one occasion, as I well remember, it was a
lift and a go, or just fetched clear. For some trifling
neglect, the captain, in company with his mate, called
me aft; a dark frown gathered on his brow as he commenced to jaw me "like the head of an old fiddle,"
said he "you want a d—n good thrashing," I replied,
"No sir; I can do better without it." Turning to the
mate who was laughing, to hide his own smile, he
ordered me to go forward. I went, and very glad was
I to improve the opportunity. Well, for so uneasy a
ship, we got along tolerably. One night in the Gulf,
heavy weather, under single reef topsails fore and aft,
our watch which was the starboard (bringing twelve
o'clock), called the larboard and went below. Had
hardly gained the forecastle before all hands were
called to double reef. It was raining hard and blowing great guns. I was on the weather of the fore-topsail and could hear the captain speaking sharply, but
could not understand what he said. Directly heard his
voice again, but still unable to comprehend his order
was in hopes that those nearer to him, in the bunt of
the sail, would be able to answer him. The third time
he spoke made up my mind that it was time some
body replied, and judging that he was only making use
of a favorite expression of his, viz: "Hurry down
there," I replied. "Aye aye, sir," finished reefing
and came down, All hands were summoned aft. "What

d—n rascal was it that answered me from that yard arm!" " 'Twas me, sir," I replied. " Why did you answer me as you did, and how many times did you hear me?" I heard you three times, but did not understand what you said, and waited for the men in the bunt to reply, till thinking you would get out of patience, I answered as if you had said " bear a hand down." " Well," said he, " I will teach you to reply to me, only, when you get ready. Now don't one of you d—n scamps put your head below decks to-night, and you, Mr. Mate, take your station on the fore scuttle, and if you permit a man to go below I will make you suffer for it." As we had no duty to perform we made a lee under the long-boat that was in her chocks on deck, and kept out of the rain. A few moments before the time arrived to go on watch again, the captain appeared on deck. Said he, " if you have come to the conclusion to answer me the next time I speak, you can go below." I told him it had always been my intention to answer him when he was understood. I thanked him for his offer now made to us, but as only a few moments remained I thought it barely worth while to go at all, and furthermore added that I guess ed we might be able to stop on deck a couple of weeks if he said so, and by that time might be in port.

A few days after, under three top-sails, jib, spanker and foresail, it becoming moderate, our wine-weaned shipmate was ordered to loose the top-gallant sails.

While in the performance of this duty, while crossing
from one yardarm to the other, the ship lurched and he
pitched over the yard. The accident was unobserved
at the time, but a loud report on the water attracted
the attention of the stevedore who was walking on the
lee-quarter-deck, which was discovered to be the striking of a Tarpaulin hat, the property of the individual
aloft; where, upon looking up, his shadow was seen
through the wet sail. The Captain immediately catching a rope, quickly got into the main-top, to find the
man clinging to the reef points of the main top-sail.
The rope was thrown over him, and in safety he was
rescued from his perilous situation. He was so strain-
ed from his over-exertion, that it was a .number of
weeks before he recovered. Fortunate was he in being
so light-weighted, or his voyage would most probably
have been ended about that time; for had he missed
the points that were so illy calculated to bear a heavy
burden, no boat that we had· was in condition to be
lowered for his rescue. Well, we kept jogging along,
sailing dull, (for the sea-clams covered our bottom, which
in those days was uncoppered) until the 25th. of
November, when we made the Capes of Virginia. Took
a pilot up the Potomac River, and on the last day
of the month arrived at Alexandria, Va., where as soon
as the ship was secured at the wharf, she was seized,
and her hatchway and gangways sealed with·red wax
and white tape, — for what cause have never yet been
able to learn. I never trod her deck again, nor did I
care to. Was paid off, receiving my discharge.

Our cook on the voyage just ended, was a white man who had been liberally educated, and for many years had taught school. His inveterate love of strong drink was the cause of his turning sailor, and on arriving at Alexandria, (his former home,) we found the desire still strong upon him. "Now boys," said he to us, "you are in want of a boarding-house; shall I procure one for you?" We accepted his kind offer, in case he found a neat and clean one. The money in which our wages were paid was the old Southern, quite valueless at the North, which we intended to get exchanged before leaving for home, as the chances might favor us. How well we succeeded the sequel will show.

Upon hearing that our friend had engaged quarters for us, our dunnage was conveyed to the place designated. Four composed our party, who were to pay three dollars per week. Arriving at the boarding-house, the landlord was consulted in regard to the disposition of our baggage &c., when a small room used for such purposes was pointed out to us, and we left it there It was between ten and eleven in the forenoon that we entered the reception room of our hotel finding it already pretty well filled with lewd women and profligate men, black and white, sailors and landsmen, some drunk and fighting, others coarsely swearing and singing the vilest productions of vice and ignorance, altogether having a jolly good time as

they termed it, and it might have been in their esti-
mation, but I thought it the toughest crew I had ever
put up with, and rather guessed the man could not
"keep a hotel." After waiting till about three o'clock,
the landlord's wife .appeared "three seas over," and
announced dinner. Taking our places at the table, we
found that the food was either burned badly or raw
entirely; for which the wife was rebuked in no very
refined language by her amiable companion. It did
not take many minutes to satisfy my appetite; or at
least to finish my attempt to do so. When the hour for
retiring approached, hoping to meet. with better
success in our lodgings than with our table fare, we
asked the Boss to show us our room. He pointed to
a garret hole, where, tumbling up a rickety stairway,
we found two beds. Pairing off, feeling pretty well
"played," we were soon under the rags of which the
bedding was composed Remembering that it was late
in the Fall, and observing that the roof overhead was
unshingled, so that moon and stars were plainly to be
seen, imagined that before morning we might possibly
be able to keep cool; this, however, was not the
case, for scarcely had we composed ourselves with the
reflection that we were out of the company so loath-
some to us, ere we were made aware of the presence
of other enemies whose friendship they were determined, .
uninvited, to thrust upon us. Who that has ever enjoyed the luxury of trying to sleep in a place infest-

ed with bed-bugs, has not some little idea of our situation? With one accord four men assembled themselves in council, and agreed that to try to sleep was a useless undertaking. Accordingly we dressed our selves in order to be ready for a skeedaddle in case affairs grew any worse, and after a long and sleeples night we left the apartment with the serious intention of finding accommodations of a superior order. Asked the landlord for the bill of our indebtedness, as we were going to leave. He only charged us three dollars each, which, taking into consideration the fact that we still lived; was not very extravagant.

I observed on going into the street, across the way, a small sign on which, on close inspection, we read, " Civil Boarding." " Here," said I to my companions, " is where we must try to get; that sign suits me much better." Over we went and knocked at the door, which was opened by a man who might have been sixty or seventy years old. We informed him that we were in quest of a boarding-house, and his sign indicating that he took boarders, we had called to see about it. " What is your occupation? " said he. " Sailors," we replied. " Oh no! on no account can I have sailor boarders,—cannot think of it for a moment. Dreadful stories are told of them, and I have two daughters in my house; it is impossible to accommodate you, you must look further. " But, " said I, " what do you take us for? Do we look like very bad men?

We stopped last night across the way, but, we don't
fancy such a place · We can behave as men, only let
us have a trial and you shall have no reason to regret
it." " Well," said he, " your leaving the other house
is a good spoke in your wheel at any rate, not supposing any place too bad for sailors." He called his
wife, we repeated what we had said to the old gent
and assured her if she would take us on trial if anything went wrong we would leave. She should be sorry,
she told us, to have bad men in the house where she
had daughters, but thought, if we would be very civil
she would take us. Very glad that we made the
change, and remained there until we started for our
northern homes. On one occasion was pained and
surprised to see one of our men somewhat elevated, in
a grog-shop ; we took him out and got him home,
fearful that our fat was now all spilled over. I told
him as we entered the house to quietly lean on me,
that we might get him to bed without the knowledge
of the inmates; but just in the wrong time he fetched
away, tumbled against the door, creating quite a sensation and bringing one of the girls to the hall. Seeing
that it could not be hid from her, I told her the story
promised her there should be no trouble, and asked
her in kindness not to let the old folks into the disagreeable secret. To this she assented, and it passed
off all right. This was the last time he was induced
to take a treat from his shipmates. We enjoyed our

stay very much, the people were very kind, and every thing was made as pleasant for us as possible.

At this early period few steamers and fewer railroads were in use for the accommodation of travellers, and the season at that particular time was so far advanced that sailing vessels, even, were hard to find on which a passage could be secured; but after some delay we found a brig of one hundred tons loading with flour and flax-seed for New York, and two of us agreed to work our passage to that port. As the money we received from our late voyage (as already intimated) was hardly redeemable at the north, and a dollar of it in scrip would nearly fill one's hat it was policy in us to exchange what we could, getting one dollar northern for two dollars of the southern. As so large a discount was unprofitable, we concluded to invest a part in flour, which I did, putting it on board the ship on freight. As the time drew near for sailing, the girls of our household were wishing us the good fortune to get frozen in, so that we should have to remain through the winter. Alas for poor human nature! they were destined to disappointment; the weather remaining moderate until we were ready for sea. As a parting gift, however, they baked up a lot of nice cakes for us to take along; which, though not required for the purpose, was a constant reminder of dear friends in a strange land. They accompanied us to the ship, and when our moorings were taken in, and the fare wells exchanged, the tears were seen to course down their cheeks "like seaweed on a clam." Under head. way, passing out of hearing, with fitting regrets we looked back to the white handkerchiefs that waved a final adieu; for we never again met, but their kindness has never been forgotten.

CHAPTER XVI.

"ON THE HOME STRETCH."

WE had a good run down the river, a fair wind and plenty of it. Coming to anchor off Port Comfort, the captain and two men went up to Norfolk, and in the fore part of next day came on board, bringing with them a small quarter of beef and half a barrel of peach brandy to wash it down with Weighed anchor, bound to Sandy Hook. The wind was free and instead of giving the vessel the proper course she hauled out to seaboard, pretty well out at that, when I made bold to ask the skipper his object in steering such a course, when he was bound for New York: "for you will never get there at this rate." I am going to get an offing; I do not wish to fetch up on the Jersey shore in case the wind comes to the eastward." Said I, "you will be glad to get hold of the land; the next change we will have a north-wester." Towards night it began to breeze on quite smartly, and it was not long before we had orders to send down the top-gallant yards, reef topsails, and take in jib; and the four men before the mast had

93

something to do. Before morning the gale took us
butt end foremost. For three days and nights we held
on as best we could, making but little headway. It
was extremely cold. Our vessel was an old bottom
that had been re-topped, the new work was too stout
for the old and badly worked where the parts met;
consequently leaked badly, and before we were aware
of the fact any quantity of water was in the hold,
which caused the flax-seed to swell by getting wet,
bursting the casks which contained it and choking the
pump boxes. Quite often were we obliged to draw
out the boxes and wash down the pumps in order to
work them at all. The ice and seed together about
the deck made it very difficult to keep our feet. So
short handed were we and the pumps going without
cessation, even when a fair wind came up we could
not be spared to make extra sail. On the fourth day,
one of the four at the pumps and attending to other
duties about the ship, was taken sick, leaving two besides myself; while our brave captain and his mate, as
drunk as beasts, were lounging in the cabin. One of
the three would usually get a little rest, while the
pumping, steering and ship-work generally were performed by the other two. When one became cold at
the wheel, he would exchange work and get warmed
up pumping, so changing back to the helm to cool off
again. Fires were not often kindled, for but little
cooking was done, peach-brandy seemed to answer

every purpose for the officers, and hard tack and raw meat was good enough for the sailors, — especially as we didn't have much labor to perform. The captain tried once to get an observation, requiring two men to keep him on his feet, but I guess the use the attempt was applied to " you might put into your eye ' without in the least obstructing the vision. Twice we made Long Island, but from lack of assistance in increasing the sail we were blown back. The last time we nearly approached Montogue Point, of which we informed the captain, and asked if we had not better put into Newport ? " " No," he growled out ; " I know your plan, you want to leave me, and then where should I be ? " He ordered us to let her run into fifteen fathoms, and tack ship ; " be sure you do not get into less than fifteen at any rate." Sick or such a cruise and about used up generally, we desired to use our own judgment and get in as soon as the wind would allow us. We spoke to the man who went below sick to come and take the wheel while we put her on the starboard tack. The wind favoring us, we lashed the wheel, gave her the jib, shook reefs out of the topsails, hoisted them up and let her run a little while, then hove her aback to sound ; not that we were very anxious to get the exact soundings, for we could guess near enough to suit us without trying, but to mislead those below and keep their suspicions quieted. Our orders were given in loud and exciting tones; so that the Captain and Mate, if awake, might imagine everything correct. "Clear away there!" "Pass the lead! "Twenty fathoms!" "all right!" "Fill away, brace the foretopsails!" &c. We let her run nearly another hour, backed foretopsail again and sounded. Got eight fathoms, but kept it to ourselves, and as the depth was passed aloud no less than twenty was reported.

The next forenoon land was seen on the larboard bow proving to be the Highlands of Neversink, on the Jersey Coast. The captain came on deck and was surprised to see land so handy to us. Said he, "Where are we now? How in the d — l did you get here?" We did not inform him that we had been keeping in smooth water along shore. Soon a Sandy Hook Pilot boat discovered us, ran quite near and hailed us, to see if we wanted a pilot. Informing the captain he replied, "If he has a Branch he can board us, if not I don't want him." Rounding too, he again asked if we wanted a pilot. "Yes, come aboard." Gaining the deck, his first words were "Call all hands and get up the to'gallant yards." we told him all hands were called. "How long have you been out?" he asked. "Sixteen days, and for twelve of them three consti- tuted "all hands.'" "'Leaking as you do, I should rather guess you have had a drag of it." The wind hauled to the eastward, and finally flattet out calm. I told the pilot we had been reefed for the whole passage; he replied that it was tough, but couldn't you get up the main-top-gallant yard ? We thought we could and did so, and set the topgallant

Just at night, got in by the hook; wind very light but fair. A little packet-sloop passed us about this time having on board an excursion party of ladies and gentlemen. Our captain, being in the condition of the Philistines on a certain occasion,—pretty well slewed—commencing to use some slang and blackguardism for his special benefit, was told by the pilot that he. had better keep his jaw to himself or he would get more than he bargained for; and in bock answers from the company he was soon made to feel like the fool that he really was.

The tide was about making against us, the pilot was was pretty well forward and ordering some one to drop the end and ascertain what the vessel was made sternway, so he that might drop the kedge-anchor under foot and hold what we had made.

I hove the lead and foundwe were going but little; throwing again and againuntil all headway was lost, and it was not long before she fell astern a trifle, of which I informed the pilot. The captain looked over the . side, and observing bubbles passing along in the current, said, "It's a damn lie; she is going three knots." The pilot came aft "on the double quick," (as soldiers say), grabbed him by the shoulders, and pitched him head and heels

down the cabin gangway, telling him he never wanted
to see his face again. "Do you think the man with
the lead-line in his hands don't know when the vessel
is going ahead or astern ? I am manager and pilot of
this craft, and if anything happens to her the respon-
sibility is mine . Furthermore, I don't wonder these
poor fellows have been sixteen days getting from the
Capes of Virginia ; My greatest surprise is that you
have ever reached where the services of a pilot are
required." Next day we arrived at New York. And
now the first thing in order was to hunt up a chance
to get home, and falling in with a Nantucket sloop I
agreed to take passage on her. The next thing was
to secure my flow ; a part of it was all we could get
at, and the sloop could not wait for us, so still remained until the balance was discovered.

Procured another chance on board a New Bedford
vessel ready to sail in a few days. Found by selling
my flour here I should save freighting it but would
have to lose one dollar on each barrel, and so concluded
to take it to New Bedford. Did so, and arrived the
next night, but to learn that no packets, or sail-boats
even, were soon to leave for Edgartown. After a
fruitless search for such a craft as seemed desirable,
we fell in with an old gentleman who was owner
of a fish-boat, with whom we concluded a bargain,
to be carried with our baggage to Edgartown, if we
would wait for a favorable time, as his boat was

quite old and rickety. We rather urged him to start immediately, as our expenses were accumlating, and our anxiety to get home was not diminishing. He told us that it was altogether unsuitable to attempt to cross Buzzard's Bay with so strong a breeze, for, said he, after getting out of the lee, it is both blowy and rugged. We still hung on for a trial, finally, telling him that if he could not go then, we should try what we could do with some other boatman. Not being a man of means, dependent on his daily earnings, it was hard to sacrifice the ten dollars in prospect, and preferring to run some risk rather than do so, said he would try it, but did not like the idea of drowning us. Well, it didn't seem to us, who had roughed it so strangely on the ocean, that there could be much danger of our drowning after getting so near home; yet many a poor sailor we might have called to mind, had perished when his own fireside warmth could almost be felt. The flour I was compelled to sell at a loss of one dollar and a quarter a barrel, concluding that my speculative genius was not of the most brilliant grade.

We got under way and headed for Wood's Hole, wind heavy and about North-west. We had proceeded but a short distance before it was necessary to shorten sail, quite a sea running, and the gale right after us. It did not require much time to make us sick of our bargain, and then we began to think what fools we were for starting; wished ourselves high and dry where

we came from. Every exertion was made by bailing to
keep the boat from sinking, while the old gent held
out the cheering assurance that as we had not yet seen
the worst of it, our minds might be made up that we
should go down, that it was impossible to weather it.
To get back was out of the question. We could carry
no sail, and were at the mercy of the waves in a boat
unseaworthy in every particular. I asked him if there
was no port to leeward, at which we might possibly
find a shelter by letting her drift. He replied, "if the
boat can live to reach it; put her dead before the
wind," and kept on bailing. We now had a foresail on
her to steady her; the spreet was taken out and the
sheet let go entirely, while the sail was allowed
to blow straight out over the bow. We got to the
entrance of a little bay, near by the remains of an old
wharf, falling however to the leeward of it, and the
boat, being unable to bear the sail necessary to reach
it, and seeing a house quite near shore, about two
miles beyond, we thought best to attempt to reach it.
We kept on until within a musket shot of the place,
and fetched up on a point surrounded by porridge ice,
which we were unable to penetrate. Wet and cold as
we were, it was certain that we could not long live on
board the boat. Taking the tiller, I sounded, and found
the ice and water would reach about to my waistband.
Overboard I went, took the old gentleman of seventy
years upon my back and landed him safely on shore;

returning, conveyed one companion in the same manner, and then the other. We then made tracks for the house, a quarter of a mile away, the snow eighteen inches on a level, and the thermometer, ranging in the vicinity of zero. Before I arrived, was as white as a tallow candle, and about as stiff. We went in. The lady of the house was an acquaintance of our old skipper, and, said she, "for Heaven's sake, Capt. Pease, where in marcy have you come from?" "Well," said he, "these young men would leave me no peace, till I would start for the Vineyard with them. A monstrous fire was in the old-fashioned fire-place, crackling and roaring in a masterly manner, and I can assure you it was the sweetest music to which I ever lent my ears. It melted me completely, as the floor around most plainly indicated, but for which the old lady protested she didn't care a whit, so long as we were making ourselves comfortable. That old fire-place, though, I never shall forget. Like many others of olden times, it should have been preserved, laid up in the archives of the nation, as a relic of its greatness, and the inexpressible comfort it afforded. Even now, as I behold its generous dimensions, capable of taking at one time a good half cord of wood, which was piled in without any regard to expense, I am led to say, in the words of a very dear friend.

"Your kindness I never can forget,
'Tis only exceeded by your extreme good looks."

The good man of the house soon after entered, and with no little surprise, asked where under the sun we came from, receiving about the same reply from our old gent as did his wife. These crazy young men over persuaded me to start for Edgartown, but as we could get nowhere else, we are compelled to throw ourselves on your hospitality. And now as we are in a good condition from the redeeming virtues of warm drink and a generous fire, we would like to have your oxen yoked. Immediately repairing to the barn, the cattle were hitched into the cart and to the shore we proceeded, got a line from the boat, made fast to the team, and with " Gee up ! " " Gee Oh ! " " Get up along there," ashore came the boat with all our baggage, which was put into the cart, and after turning the boat over, for better preservation, was taken to the house, anticipating a tarry there from the general look around us, it still snowing hard and freezing fast. The old gentleman was feeling uneasy, fearful that his board would more than overrun the amount to be received, thinking strongly of footing it the next day around the foot of the bay, frequently calling himself a fool for getting into such a scrape. His better judgment prevailed, and it was considered worse than useless to attempt it. Thus do the aged sometimes learn that experience is a teacher still. We told him, however, to make himself comfortable, that his expenses would be attended to by us ; whereupon he became more reconciled.

In a few days the weather became tolerably good, but still. blowing something of a breeze. We told our hospitable friends not to do for us˙ anything out of their usual way, as we would like moderate fare, on account of the length of our purses, but that we wished to pay them for all the trouble we caused. Rising very early a short time after, was pleased to find a bright starlight morning, with not a breath of wind moving. Called all hands, got ready for a start, conveyed our dunnage to the shore, reballasted the boat hitched on the cattle, and soon (after paying our bills,, which were much less than we˙expected,) were rowing for dear life towards home, with our skipper at the helm. The prospect of soon greeting the loved ones lent additional strength and muscle to our efforts, and over the water we flew like a thing of life, almost forgetting the old hulk which had so nearly proved our coffin. It continued calm until near the harbor entrance, when the wind hauled out North-east and a snow-storm set in. We kept on and struck her on the shore between the wharves, got out our property and with the help of friends at hand, hauled the boat up and turned her over. Sent our skipper to the Tavern, promising to settle his keeping.

For a month or more the weather was about as bad as needs be, cold, blowey, snowing, and a considerably bad time generally. About this time a man was landed from a vessel, who wanted a passage to New Bedford

We waited upon Capt. Pease, paid him for the services rendered us, and engaged him to take the passenger. When ready to stårt, by our assistance the boat was put into the water and all preparations for sailing generally attended to ; we then bade him farewell. Learned afterwards that he arrived safely, but I never saw him again. Glad enough to be once more at home, had saved some money, by which I was enabled to make a few little presents to the friends I so often had entertained fears of never more meeting.

> "Home again, home again,
> From a foreign shore,
> And Oh ! it fills my heart with joy,
> To meet my friends once more

CHAPTER XVII.

FTER remaining about home, attending to the spring fishing at the south side of the Vineyard, on the first day of May, started after a ship which was to be fitted for a whaling cruise, being the first one that our Islanders had ever put into that business. I was already under partial agreement to go as mate of a coaster, when I met Capt. Jethro Daggett, who informed me that they had concluded the bargain for a ship, of which he was to have the command, and he wished me .to go the voyage in her. At first I refused, telling him of my engagement, and that my wages, were to be twenty-five dollars per month. His reply was, " You had far better go with me ; you will realize much more on a voyage whaling, than in the coasting business." He talked so much that finally, like a great fool, I said I would go. Said he, " I wish you to be on hand to go to New Haven and assist in bringing the ship here. Accordingly on the first of May, 1816 in company with a boat's crew took a whale boat, our second mate in charge, and started. Got up to Vine yard Haven, (or, as it was then called,) Holmes' Hole, and a fresh westerly wind drawing down the Sound, thought best to land, which we did, near the entrance of the harbor, at a place called Frog Alley. Stopped with a man named David Dunham, as too much wind prevailed to proceed. After getting dinner, some of our party concluded to go up to the village to see the fashions, and have a chat with the girls; for at that time, as now, they enjoyed the reputation of being quite sociable, intelligent and agreeable. Changing our clothing, a little ambitious to make as favorable an impression as possible, we fancied, (scanning our good looks,) that we would " pass in a crowd." Whether it was the hope of meeting such a reception as I had pictured, or wish to show my companions my agility, has never been fully decided in my own mind; yet from some cause I did undertake to try an experiment which proved both very silly and extremely injurious.

For the benefit of you who are listening to me, I will relate how it turned out, hoping from experience, a lesson may be imparted, leading you, in all the affairs of life to " look before you leap." In front of the house, on a line with the hill running parallel with the shore, was a high board fence. Thinking the nearest way round was to jump over it, gathering myself for a good start I dashed along, throwing my full strength into the leap. The fence was cleared, but not so the crumbled wall of an old cellar on which I landed. Instead of the green sward on a level with the fence, as I imagined, I went to the bottom of a· pit fifteen feet deep, and found the rocks hard and flinty. My ankle bone was split open, and numerous other slight wounds on various parts of my body led me to postpone my intended visit indefinitely. I didn't care for any new clothes that day. Was helped up to the house and the old lady kindly fixed me up as best she could. My comrades told me I might as well give up the cruise and take a carriage home, but I told them No; I had begun it, and was going through if I lived. A salve was furnished me, and in the morning we started, the men helping me along; quite reluctantly, however, for as the foot was quite badly swollen, they were fearful of the result if I kept on. With my foot elevated to to the thwart in front of me, I assisted in rowing the boat, until getting out of the mouth of the Sound, saw a schooner ahead, we sailed and rowed together and gained up with her considerably, when we fired several muskets as a signal for her to heave to. When near enough to hail, was asked what we wanted. We asked where he was bound. He replied, " New York." Being asked for a tow, " Yes, come aboard," said he. We did so, dropping the boat astern. Found that the captain was a cripple as well as myself, having a broken shoulder received from the main gaff the night before. We were towed to Block Island, then left the vessel in a calm. Our boat reached Black Point, a little west of New London, where we landed. The provisions laid in for our cruise consisted of a bag of hard-bread. Taking some of it we went up to a house, where we were invited in by a young lady, who informed us that her parents were at church, it being Sunday. Told her we would like some milk to go with our bread, whereupon she set out the table with a large pan of rich looking milk, with bowls to put it in for each, and started for what appeared to be the parlor, forgetful that bread and milk was difficult to eat with one's fingers. She apologized and brought on the spoons, but when we afterwards perceived a young man, doubtless her lover ("Sparking" Sunday afternoon), she was readily excused. We finished our meal and asked her charge, after holding a consultation with the young gent, she informed us it was two dollars. Didn't dispute the bill, but thought it rather steep.

Started afresh, not much wind, but rowed until night, then put into a little harbor and lodged on board a coaster. Next morning made another start, still using "white-ash" for a breeze. Stopped next about noon in a nice little harbor called Sachem's Head. Here we found a public house, and had a good meal the first since leaving Holmes Hole; thence continued on, arriving at New Haven just at night.

The ship was in sight, all rigged, very nicely painted, her main deck chrome yellow, quarter-deck prussian blue, and as gay as a ribbon all over. She did look about the nicest of any vessel I had then ever looked upon. I am thus particular in describing her outward

appearance, so that as you find out more of her qua,-
ities you may be able to judge how very deceitful
appearances are sometimes found to be. The new purchasers paid fourteen thousand dollors for her, and
supposed they were buying a new vessel. Found the
mainmast had to be taken out on account of being rotten, the original owners paying the expenses. We
took thirteen cords of wood for ballast, and most of
the casks for our whaling voyage. They were of very
poor staves, thin heads, too small, hoops so thin the
rivet-heads would draw out while being driven.

Started for home in one week, and arrived after
three days passage. She was fitted at Mayhew's wharf.
A few days before we were ready for sea, while at
work on the quarter-deck, I overheard a conversation
between Captain Daggett and Mr. Peter Coffin, who
was going our chief mate. "Captain D.," said Mr.
Coffin, we are too old to go whaling, we ought not to
go." Says Capt. D., "Oh no; I feel smart and active,
am only about sixty, just in my prime." "But," said
Mr. C., "I am obliged to go; if I had your property
I should remain on shore." Capt. D. said, "Well,
neither you nor I will stand any watch on the voyage;
unless sometime when we may be running in for the
land, or in some other special emergency. We shall
have plenty of younger man and boys to do the watch
standing. Mr. C. replied, "I shall always stand my
watch." He did and stood it like a man, keeping

wide awake himself and all the rest of us; there was no sleeping in his watch on deck, "nary time." In farther conversation Mr. C. observed, "We have too many green boat-steerers, I don't like them, they lack experience." They are just what I wanted," said Capt. D., "I wish to break them in my way; then they will be good for something." Strange idea, thought I, A few weeks passed, and in such order as she was, we were ready to sail for the coast of Africa, on a fourteen months cruise. Having cleared from the Custom House the night previous, we set sail on 5th of July, 1816.

CHAPTER XVIII.

S previously stated, the Apollo was the first ship of a long list subsequently sent out by the people of Edgartown. Feeling quite independent from the effects of the previous day, our National Anniversary, it was decided not to take a Pilot, our mate being competent to act as such. As the wind was from the westward, in was deemed best to go through the ship channel, over the shoals, making our course to the eastward of Georges Banks. Got along finely, the wind and tide both favoring us, the wind increasing in the afternoon of the first day, but still fair. At eight o'clock pumped ship. Found plenty of water in the lower hold; pumped a long time without freeing her, and after a while the pumps became choked with chips and gravel. We hoisted them out, drew the boxes, and with long poles drove out the snags. Replaced them, but it was not long before they were again choked, when they were again taken out and served as before. Slung a man under the arms, and lowered him into the pump-well, with a basket to gather up the

111

kindling stuff. He, reported any quantity of it, while bucket-full after bucket-ful of all kinds of dirt was sent up. Directly he sang out for the end of a rope to be sent down, as he had found something as large as a man's body. He bent on to it, and up we hauled a good-sized piece of rotten timber. Sent down the rope again as he ordered, and away came up another of the same kind! In great surprise it was asked, "Where can they have come from? Is he going to bend on the ships bottom?" We thought we were in a new ship, as it had been so represented, and now timber thirty years old was making its mysterious appearance. But the secret was soon out when we learned that she had been an old Horse Jockey, formerly known as the "Henry," had made forty voyages to the West Indies and was afterwards fitted up for the purpose of selling; and those who bought her did get most egregiously sold. After a while, having got the well all cleared, we in pump, and to pumping again, but did not gain much on her. Headed her for Boston, sharp hauled on the wind. Soon began to lessen the water in the hold, which proved the leak high up, somewheres forward. Kept off again, thinking that perhaps the next day we might find the leak. Let her drive, going along first rate.

Ten days out, early in the morning, raised a large sperm-whale and lowered for him, but being all green hands in the boat, the whale was gallied. He would have stowed down eighty barrels, but escaped us. About noon another large fellow was raised, and now the captain was going to show the "greenies" how to do it. He soon got up with him. The whale had some white spots on him, and as he took a notion to whirl round that he might have a fair view of the Capt. and his boat, opening his mouth at the same time (probably to laugh), the old gent was terribly frightened and sang out, "Stern all! stern all, boys! 'tis a rogue whale, and he will eat the boat! See the white spots on him!" Having seen all he cared to of us, he went down and we saw no more of him, while we returned to the ship again. Had hardly got alongside when the mate said, "For God's sake Capt. Daggett, why didn't you strike that whale? You were near enough." He replied, "The whale didn't act as I should have liked, but if my boat-steerer had been a man of experience I should have tried him," Mate replied, "That is just what I told you; we didn't want any of your d—n green boat steerers."

Towards night the third whale was in sight, right ahead. We down with two boats; I bowed the mate's; the other boat came up to the whale first. "Give it to her" was the word. The boat-steerer let go his iron, striking a place of slack blubber, which bent the iron but did not enter. Darted again, and his iron entered just enough to cover one flue, and the line coming taut, it drew out. The Mate's boat now came

alongside, and he sang out to the boatsteerer, "dart!"
He did dart, or rather pitchpoled his iron about half
way to the whale. Told him to give him the other
iron; he did, and away it went twenty feet into the
water beyond. By this time the greasy fellow thought
it about time to make himself scarce, thinking perhaps by and by somebody might accidently hit him.
So off he went, four irons hove at him and not a
blood fetched! The boatsteerer, Lem. Kelley by name,
was as stout as a giant, and as clever and lazy a
fellow as ever lived. When we got on board, and the
boats hoisted up, another row among the officers and
Kelly followed. Says the mate to Kelly, "Why didn't
you fasten to that whale?" "When I stood up, I
was so scared I didn't know whether I was darting
an iron or was being chawed up by an alligator."
Said he was an old sea-dog, had been in the merchant
service, but had never been whaling before, and never
was frightened as that monster frightened him. "I
never wish to see any more whales, and what is
more, I want my discharge at the very first port we
enter, for I shall be of no use here I am perfectly
satisfied."

We cruised near the coast of Guinea some little
time, but saw no whales and as the land did not appear more than eight or ten miles distant, a boat
was ordered on shore for fruit. Throwing into her a
part of a porpoise caught the day before, some old

spikes, hoops, and worn-out knives, a few old cast-off duds, started for the shore. The wind was light and the ship did not have much way. We rowed and rowed, until the ship was hull down, the land being over twenty instead of ten miles away when we left her. Getting in shore, saw a little village of huts or wigwams, toward which we pulled. It was rough-landing on account of the surf. An old man, who proved to be the Chief, came out and made signs for us to land more to the eastward. Finally he belched out in very loud tones, which was interpreted by us to mean "come on." The boat striking the beach, a simultaneous rush was made by the natives, number-ing from three to five hundred, who came from over the hill, and taking the boat up bodily, men and all, conveyed us to the woods, quite a distance from high-water mark.

These people were as naked as they were born into the world, except the Chief who had some rags tied around his body. He inquired of us if we were a war-ship crew, making himself intelligible to us by pointing to the ship, and then imitating as best he could the noise of a cannon. It so happened that near where we landed was the bleached scalp of an old whale, we replied to his question by calling his attention to it, and then taking the attitude of strik-ing him with an iron, he appeared satisfied, fully comprehending our acts. Trading then commenced.

There was an abundance of fruit of different kinds,
and as the natives made their selections from the valu-
bles displayed, we had only to indicate by marks
in the sand how much we wanted of the different
fruit, which was immediately placed in the boat. We
were probably the first white persons ever visited them.
They inspected us closely, shoving up our sleeves,
and pantaloon legs to see if we were white, thinking
our faces were painted. They would not suffer any
of us to go to the village.

It was now calm, the ship had drifted entirely out
of sight, and we were beginning to feel rather un-
comfortable, among a horde of savages and perfectly
helpless just at night our eyes were gladdened by a
view of the ship, approaching with a light breeze.
We made signs that we wished to leave, but the old
Chief would not let us. We kept an eye on our boat
hatchet and knives, determined, if they did attack
us, to sell our lives at a good price, meanwhile
could hardly make out their intentions toward us.
These people were finely formed, straight as an
arrow, the men very tall and massive in their build,
black as jet, the skin shining like a piece of ebony.
All ages were represented, from the papoose a few
days old to men and women who might have been
a hundred and forty, with heads as white as the
driven snow.

The children were carried in a sort of basket,

formed by the bark of a tree doubled up and attached
to the shoulders, from which position, from the
peculiar formation of the female, the little ones could
easily receive from their mothers their nourishment.

The ship ran in as near as it was safe, hauled
aback, ran the colors up and down, while we were
endeavoring to get away. At last we made signs to
the Chief, if he would let us go on board, when the
sun arose again would return with lots of good things.
This seemed to suit his ideas very well, and telling
us to get in on top of the fruit, such a gathering
to get a hand on our boat was never seen before.
Up she was taken, and toward the shore was being
quickly borne, when a scream from one of the girls
caused each one to let the boat drop. It appeared
that Lem, the fellow who didn't like whales, attempted to kidnap the girl, or was trying to frighten
her; but it came near turning our fat all into the
fire. They appeared greatly exasperated, and for a
while we didn't know how 'twould turn out. With
considerable coaxing, however, the boat was again
raised and launched, and taking our oars we made the
best time possible toward the ship, glad enough to
be out of their reach. We did not go ashore when
the sun arose next morning. The Captain was badly
frightened and never expected to see us again; seemed
real glad when we were safe on board, but no more
than were we to be there ourselves. Soon left the
coast, not having seen a spout.

Although previous to leaving home the mate had
been told by Capt. D. that he would not be required
to stand watch, yet so far he had, just as regular as
clock work. But to show how much was meant by the
captain's pretentions, a little incident will suffice. I
was in the mate's watch. He had just asked how
much the hour-glass lacked of being out. (In those
days no clocks were used.) 1 told him ten minutes,
said he, "I believe a few-minutes rest before going below will not hurt me," and taking a stool sat down on
it near the cabin sky-light, which was open. The
captain, observing it, came out of the cabin in a perfect
tempest, and charged him with being asleep in his
watch on deck. Mr. C. denied that he had slept a
wink, saying that it was only five minutes by the glass
since it was consulted for him. "If I have been asleep
it was a d——n short one. He got up and gave the
chair a hurl against the bulwarks that completely de
molished it, whereupon the captain threatened to land
him the first port he made.

After leaving the coast, cruised along toward Rio
Janeiro. One day about noon, had been taking the sun.
I was alone in the steerage, a small door between that
and the cabin being open, captain and mate came down.
Captain asked Mr. Coffin what his Latitude was ; he
told him, when the captain said, "You are wrong ;
Mr. Godfrey's is so-and-so, and yours must be incor-
rect, some mistake somewhere," "I tell you," said

Coffin, "I am right. D—n Godfrey, I don't go by his reckonings; I go by my own." The next thing I heard was the clattering of the crockery, and somebody fall on the floor. The table for dinner was spread out' and the chests occupied most of the floor room. I thought I would go and see what the matter was. There they were, having a nasty hook, captain and mate clenched, the mate crammed down behind the chests, Mr. Coffin had one hand on the captain's breast, and with the other had him by the ear, both looking rather savage. Mr. C. gave a pull on the ear, which split it up about an inch the blood flowed freely from it, saying, "I'll never give up to no 'Old Doggett' so long as there's a drop of old Betty Martin runs through my veins. Captain Daggett, seeing me standing by the door, cried out, "Take this d—n rascal away from me;" but as no names were called, I left suddenly, not caring to get mixed up in the affair. About this time the captain's son came down with the dinner, and seeing the encounter, set it on the table and called the second mate and boatsteerers to the assistance of his father, and soon they were separated. At about two o'clock P. M., another row was kicked up between the second mate and a boatsteerer on the port bow, which the captain saw and put a stop to. I began to think that fighting was better attended to than whaling and wished that I had gone coasting rather than on this voyage.

Not long after, in the latter part of the day, a large
ship was seen bearing down to us, seeming to want to
speak us. We hove aback our main-topsail and he
passed our stern, running under our lea, and parted his
wheel-rope. She luffed right up alongside, stove two
of her boats, but the yards did not get foul. She
proved to be an English transport loaded with emi-
grants, who crowded her sides and rigging to get a
sight of us. She fell of to leeward, striking our fashion
piece into his quarter galley, which was stowed with
crockery; an opening was made, out of which at
least two cart loads were dumped into the ocean. As
she was bound into Rio we agreed to keep company,
both arriving three days after. Our ship still leaked
badly in heavy weather. The captain told Mr. Coffin
to get his duds ready to leave, as he was going to
discharge him Mr. C. told him he did not like to leave
there, as all were strangers to him and he had no
money. He was told that it made no odds; if he did
not go of his own accord he would have a file of soldiers to help him along. Mr. C. replied, " Rather than
be dragged by soldiers, I will go." He got ready
and put his things in the boat. Before he left he told
us we would have to go either to Brazil Banks, Right-
whaling, or Cape Horn sperm whaling, but by all
means to be in favor of going to the Cape. The captain then ordered him to leave, adding that if any
other man or boy wished to go he was at liberty to

do so. The boat left with Mr. Coffin. One boatsteerer said, as there was to be so much fighting on board he thought best to leave, for if he remained he should be obliged to do his part. The captain replied. If you are a fighting character you had better, for I prefer to do all the fighting done here. Accordingly he left. The next day I applied for my discharge, but after some hard words passing between us, finally gave it up, preferring to suffer some myself, rather than as he said, be the means of breaking up the voyage; for if I left, the rest of the ships crew were determined to follow me. Afterwards, when on shore, made another attempt to hold him to his agreement in regard to discharging any who wished to go, but he protested so, that I should ruin him, that he would be compelled to sell the ship, &c., the tears filling his eyes on account of it, that my naturally sensitive nature was touched to such a degree that the thought of leaving was abandoned, with his promising to act more as a man should toward his fellow man. I have no doubt, that had I left the ship, when I got home every old woman would have been down on me.

In the afternoon all hands were taken to the Custom House, the captain trying to prove Mr. Coffin a very troublesome man, and wishing us to give in evidence to that effect. I imagined his object, and told the boys, if they had to make any statements, to say as few words as possible and be wholly on their guard.

Underneath the Custom House was a grog-shop, into
which we were all invited by the captain, who called
for all kinds of liquors and told all hands to help
themselves, as it was his treat. "Come on, my boys;
now don't be shy because the Old Man is free with
his rum. Here Ripley, step up don't refuse." I took
a very light glass, but not so with quite a number;
before their craving was satisfied they were ready for
most anything. A few were allowed to go into the
office at a time, while the others were making merry
at the Old Man's expense. When not observed, I
slipped out and dodged around the corner, and forgot
to report myself until the business was all finished,
keeping shady till there was a mustering in the vicinity of the boat, when I went down to return with the
rest to our ship. The captain asked me where I had
been? I answered him evasively by telling a white lie,
that I stepped out and got lost, and could not find
my way back until it was to late. Capt. D., said
he was very sorry, as my boat had already left the
shore; told me to get into his, and go on board
with him. Said I, "I don't belong to your boat,
nor do I ever wish to put foot on the ship again."
After a while we shoved off. For recruits, twenty-
five bushels of corn was purchased, also some fresh
beef. The corn was inhabited; every kernel was a
tenement, and every tenement had a good sized white
worm in it. The beef was in an awful condition;

being killed the night before, it was brought to market on the greasy backs of naked women, while the perspiration of their over heated bodies and the blood of half-dressed bullocks were beautifully mingled together. It was enough to make a sensible dog sick to his stomach.

In a few days went to sea, a constant lookout being kept at our mast-heads for whales, but did not raise any. The next land-fall made was the island of Ascension, near St Helena. We went in, and sent a boat ashore for Green Turtle, but as the season was rather late, were disappointed by not getting any, they having laid their eggs and returned to their ocean home. But if the turtle had not been any better than we got in the earlier part of the voyage, it would have been no great loss. I neglected to state in the proper place, that we made for our first port the island alluded to. We ran in there, stopped only a few hours, landed and captured five very large turtle, got them off to the ship all right, cooked one and found him as tough as a shark and as strong as Goliah. The others were left to roam about under foot on deck. To prevent them from getting overboard, iron rails were lashed a long where the ship was not coiled up, (in those days it was not the practice to coil the bulwarks the whole length of the vessel), As I was saying, irons were used as rails to prevent the escape of our animals; but one dark

night somebody let the lower rail down, and in the
morning they were among the missing. We did not
cry over it, but our captain was considerably grieved,
thinking no doubt, if they were too tough for cabin
use they might do for sailors. But to return to Ascension. A war brig, called the Leverett, belonging to
the English navy, was anchored there, and thirty men
belonging to her had taken possession of the island.

The night before we got in it was blowing hard, and
a rough sea running; our lower bob-stay, an eight
inch rope, was pitched in two pieces. When we came
to an anchor, a number of spars were secured under
our bow for staying, from which necessary repairs could
be made upon the stay, and search made for the leak.
After unserving the end of the bob-stay leading into
the stern, in examining the hole from where it came
out, an augur hole was discovered leading into it,
which proved the place that had caused us so much
touble and hard labor, — for pumping is no holiday
amusement. This hole had been overlooked when the
ship was undergoing repairs previous to her being sold
for a whaler, and the secret was out in regard to her
only leaking when before the wind ; it then being slack,
the water could find its way in, but when a strain
was on the opening was closed up by the stay. With
a good lot of oakum we made it all right, and it
didn't trouble us any more.

Fitted the stay and lethered it, shaved the inner end

and rove it, and set it up taut with a watch tackle; then had a chance to go on shore. We found the island very rocky, and every foot of land seemed infested with rats, who did not appear to be at all alarmed at our presence: guess they were not aware what uncivil things men could be. They acted as if they enjoyed themselves hugely, sometimes hiding their eyes in the crack of the rocks, or under a bunch of Parsley. Thinks I. What a delightful country for John Chinaman!

We came very near getting a large lot of goats should have succeeded, but they were more accustomed to the method of travelling about there, and rather outwitted us on several occasions. Once we had, as we supposed, a number cornered, all ready to put our hand on them, but as in the case of the Irishman's flea, we put our hands where they were and they weren't there! Up they went, out of reach, where, on a rock not much larger than a man's hand, they looked and grinned at us in defiance.

With a fair wind soon started for Cape Horn. Cruised along without seeing any whales, winds varable, no regular gales, but quite strong blows, and little of all kinds. As we neared the Cape the weather grew worse. Sent down top gallant yards and masts fore and aft. Rigged in jibboom, took in the sprect sail yard, unrigged the spanker altogether, and bent a small storm mizzen. Getting pretty well up to Staten Island, the weather moderated. One day, about two o'clock, a large sperm whale was seen about a third of a mile distant, off the starboard beam. The captain, as usual, was taking his *siesta* in his bunk below. The mate called and informed him that a whale was quite handy to us, and asked if he might get out a couple of boats. "Yes," he replied. We began to unlash when he came upon deck, ordered us to hold on as it was no use. "We're in too high latitudes to kill whales; if we should strike a whale before morning, we should be forced to give him up." So we gave up the chance, the whale remaining in sight till dark; fine weather all night and a beautifull day followed it. We kept dragging along, and at last weathered Cape Horn. Ran down on whaling ground on the coast of Peru, having enjoyed quite a quiet time, only an occasional dispute arising which was settled without resorting to kicks and cuffs. For some time saw no whales, and were getting out of patience; but as I was on the lookout aloft one day I caught sight of a fellow right ahead and sang out, "There she blows!" "Where away" was asked. I replied, "There goes flukes, right ahead sir." "Clear away the boats," the Captain ordered. Two boats lowered, which were commanded by the Captain and Mate. The captain's boat got fast, and instead of killing the whale himself, as he should, he let the boatsteerer throw the lance which was boned, the whale rolled, the line came taut, and the boat was capsized. The mate immediately fastened, and soon the whale was spouting thick blood. We felt better as we beheld his corps. Towed him to the ship and went to work cutting him in. It was now the first of March, 1818; nine months from home, and we hadn't .taken oil enough to burn in the binnacle lamp. After this whales were quite plenty, but only two at a time were allowed to be brought to the ship and only one if it was near night. All hands being green, it made very bad work cutting in. Large wooden wedges were used for the purpose of keeping the blubber lifted, resembling those used in splitting large logs of wood. It took us the greater part of a day to get a fifty barrel fellow in. Here we took about three hundred barrels in three months, lived hard, short rations and of the meanest kind. A common dish was corn and worms pounded up together, made into soup, with a very small piece of salt meat cooked in it. Had some fish which we cooked when the opportunity was afforded, refusing none except sharks; but sometimes we were sharkish enough to try them. We took out on the voyage forty-three barrels of meat, while in later days three hundred is not considered extravagant. Many a time when it was served up, I have taken my allowance at a single bite; yet I never had the reputation of having a very large swallow, and several times in my life have come quite near choking to death because

my swallow was so small. The bread was very good,
but less than half a pound was to go with our morsel
of meat for the twenty-four hours. The only fault with
the bread was, not enough of it. We soon got sick
fo samp, it was sour and musty and often the top of
the pot in which it was boiled would be covered with
the worms. One day it came down presenting its
usual appearance, not fit for a decent hog to eat, and
I was detailed to take the kid in which it was to the
captain. I asked him if he thought it was fit to feed
men on? I had told the men, prior to my going aft
that it would kick up a row but if every man would
follow me I would go. Instead of that, not a man
stood by me; but I kept on with it. He replied to
my question by saying it was good enough Said I,
"We cannot agree with you." He called me a muti-
nous rascal, and asked why I was the only one to find
fault. I told him they had all agreed to follow me and
defend their rights, but had deceived me. The bread
was usually served out fourteen cakes per week, but
not unfrequently we were cheated out of a part of our
allowance by not getting it until the eight day; this
was the case on the present occasion, our bread being
due the day previous, and I told him so. He denied
the assertion and ordered me forward, promising me
(not the bread but) to land me on the first desolate
island they arrived at. Told him that did not frighten
me. "Then," said he, I will put you on board the

first man o'-war we speak." Said I, "That will be
better than remaining here to starve, for I shall get
semething to eat. He got pretty well out of humor
and scolded dreadfully I told him all that we wanted
was our rghts" "What do you want." "Sir, if we
are to have fourteen cakes of bread per week, we want
it, and want it when it is due." Said he, "You are.
not on allowance." I replied that he was correct
"You not do give half an allowance. I wish to know,
sir, if we are to have such a quantity dealt out at a
stated time, and the time is allowed to overrun
twenty-four hours, if there is not an occasion for complaint?" All this time not a man came aft to my assistance. I told him finally that I was hungry and
wanted my bread and must have it. The bread was
usually headed up on the quarter deck, and at this
time a number of casks stood there. He spoke to the
mate who had taken Mr. Coffin's place, asking if that
was the day for serving out the bread. Not wishing
to disagree with the captain, he replied "I believe it
is." At last, finding that I was not to be scared or
beaten out of it, he ordered the cooper to get his tools
and open his cask "for this "gentleman," as he sar-
castically called me. I often laugh when thinking about it; but it was provoking. "Now," said he,
"you can get your bread bag and call the others for
theirs." I replied that as for getting mine, I was ready
to, but the others might stay and starve if they choose

to; I should not call them. A boatsteerer usually did
the counting. The captain asked if I had not better
watch him for fear of being cheated. I replied that
there would be no harm in it, and did so. He completed the task for all the crew, and a large sack was
passed up for the cabin supply. Previous to this time
the bread for the cabin always held out much longer
than ours forward, and we judged the reason why was
that they drew a much larger quantity, which without
doubt was the case. " Now," said the captain, " hadn't
you better have an eye out to see that he doesn't put
in more for the cabin than belongs there?" "Yes
sir," I responded, "there is need enough of doing just
that very thing; for it is not doubted that it has been
done more than once." I did watch, and that time it
went in all correct; when I said. "For one, I agree
that no bread will be required for the steerage, or
asked for, till the cabin allowance is gone. And sure
enough, theirs was all gone two days before we were
out. I was in the mate's boat and watch.
We always agreed quite well, and a short time after
the circumstances just alluded to occurred, in our watch
on deck, the mate told me that not a great while be
fore, the captain told him that I was just right about
the bread; that he know it all the time; meant to give
it to me, but was only trying to see if he couldn't
make me back down, and that the crew were as mean
as the d—l to back out and leave me in the scrape

alone. " But he hung well," he added. That acknowledgment made him look to me worse than ever. What
good it did him to tease me, even against his own
convictions of right and justice, was a puzzle to me.

But to proceed with the cruise. The captain, thinking
a supply of wood and water necessary, headed her for
Tombez Mr. Godfrey, who was Chief Navigator and
ship keeper, was sick below. After several days made
the land, and, not being familar with the coast, ran by
the port thirty-three miles to leaward. Came to anchor
off the mouth of a river, and went ashore, but soon
found by its being salt that it was not the one we were
in quest of. Found several others, but still none that
answered our purpose. Spent the day roaming around.
and at night went on shipboard. Next day was also
used up in fruitless attempts to find fresh water; but
there was no lack of mosquitoes and sand-flies, — they
almost devoured us. Disheartened and hungry, joined
the ship again late at night At noon of the past
day, Mr. Godfrey had been on deck and taken an observation, and informed us that thirty-five miles to the
southward lay the river we wished to find. We took a
boat and started for it. On reaching it, in order to
enter, had to cross a very rugged sand-bar. The
boat broached to and partly filled with water, the
steering oar broke off the sternpost, but steering with
the other oars we finally got over and entered the
river all right ; still doubtful whether it was Tombez

or not, until tasting the water was convinced   Had
we been acquainted with the kind of animals it furnished
we might have known at once, as the alligators
were as thick as June-bugs. The next morning with a
pilot returned to the ship. Got her under way, and at
night of the following day let our anchor go off the
mouth of the river. Our boats were sent for wood and
water. There was any quantity of wood of various
kinds, the Mangrove most common. Our casks were
filled, rolled into the river, lashed together and towed
by the boats.

Some of our oil was sold here for sweet potatoes
and sugar. The sugar was pressed in large cakes
and had the appearance of maple sugar, it being quite
dark colored. It was packed in flags braided together.
The pilot who brought us up the coast was owner of
a small brigantine, and did some trading along the
coast. For that purpose we sold him two sixty gallon
casks of black fish oil, though he supposed it was
sperm, as it had been represented to him as such.
Also sold him fifty fathoms of second hand tow line
for a cable for his craft ; by doubling it was all sufficent,
as his vessel was only about ten tons. He immediately
started for Guayoquil for a market. He did not go
up to the wharf, but anchored outside. Humpback
whales were very plenty about there ; in the night it
was discovered that his vessel was on the move, which
proved to be one of those saucy fellows who had got

afoul of the cable and was making off with the vessel, but the line crossways of the craft brought her on her beam ends, when the line parted, he taking the greater portion of it for his part. But this was not to be the end of our pilots misfortunes. He afterwards went up to dispose of his oil, and was landing or getting it hoisted to land, when, high enough to swing off, the tackle parted, letting the cask fall on the one beneath it, staving both and saving but little which was scooped up with dirt and water. When he returned from the unprofitable cruise, his lamentable story was told, and our sympathies were expressed in the only way that was in our power : such as we had gave,we unto him, while the captain replaced the tow-line with a new one.

After procuring all the wood and water required we shipped a man by the name of Young, who said he was a carpenter and had been cast away ; was just able to work his way down from Panama, and was anxious to get away from Tombez. We left for the off shore ground, and took a few whales.

• One afternoon raised a large English Whaler running down for us. The man recently shipped was standing at the mast-head, looking for whales. As the ship neared us he came down, complained of an attack of fever and ague, and must go below. The ship hove her yards aback, and our captain was invited on bo ard One boat s crew boarded her. It was near night. The

English carpenter we had shipped was only pretending
sickness, and he · began to own up that he, with five
others, had run away from that ship with everything
they could take with them, Said he, " They have seen
me with their spy-glass, and no doubt recognized me,
while aloft." He was in a peck of trouble for fear of
being returned to the ship he had deserted, thinking
he would be carried to England and hung. The En
glish Captain asked if we had been in port of late,
and was told that we had just left Tombez. " Did
you ship any man,,' he continued! " Yes," was replied, "one who called himself an Englishman."
"What kind of a looking man was he?" Our captain
thoughtlessly gave a good description of him " He
is my man," replied the Englisman ; our officers saw
him aloft and recognized him, I shall come after him
to-morrow." " Well, sir," said Capt. Daggett, "if he
belongs to you I suppose you will have to get him;
I cannot prevent you." Late at night the boat came
back. Capt. D. called the man up and questioned
him ; asked him why he lied to him? To which he
replied, " You are a gentleman, and if I had owned
up to being a runaway sailor you would not have
shipped me. " Well," said he in reply, " he is coming after you to-morrow." We pitied the poor fellow,
knew it would go hard with him, and it was determined to avoid his going back if it was possible to
prevent it.

The boatsteerers on our ship were gentlemen boat-steerers, not having any watch to stand and doing generally, about as they saw fit. The crew were divided into three watches, usually four men to each. I told the boys in our watch, if it were possible we must run away from the English ship. At eight o'clock took my trick at the wheel, and soon after a little squall of rain and mist made it so dark that the other ship was hid from view. Preceiving this, the helm was clapped up, and kept her dead before the wind without starting the sheets. Were under short sail, and had been on the wind. When we kept off were only about a third of a mile apart. Kept the yards braced as before, so that she would show up as little as possible, supposing that the Englishman would keep on his course and pass us. But to our disappointment, when it lighted up his jibboom was almost over us; he had missed us, and judging that we were to leeward, had made his calculations just right to outwit us. But we came the square on him in the end. I still let her run as I had done, steering pretty widely to lead him to think we were indifferent what course was made. No chance offered for us to escape him; when we were relieved by the other watch, I told them to get away from him if they could. No chance offered during that watch. The third watch took the deck, and the wind died away to a calm. In the morning he was two or three miles on our lee quarter, wind light, and we outsailed him, but in the afternoon a breeze sprang up, when he began to draw upon us. By and by up went his colors as a signal for us to heave to. At first no notice was taken of them, but after he kept making signals, thought best to heave aback and let him come up. Was now only half a mile off. "Now," said I to our new man, "you haul off your duds in less than no time and put mine on instead. He wore a red shirt and blue pants, and for a hat he had a Pati with a brim a foot wide. "Tell me," said I, just the same story you told the captain when he shipped you." He did so, and then I told him to make himself scarce,—down to the keelson of the hold if he liked. I was now Matthew Young. Turning to the Captain, said I. "If you want Matthew Young, I am he." The whole was clear to his vision, and judging from his appearance he approved of it. After Young went below I busied myself in the waist, planing a broken oar for a lance-pole. Just before the boat arrived I left it and went aft; told the boys not to betray me, I was going to turn in, had a severe attack of fever and ague.

It was not long before the old Englishman rolled in over the lee quarter rail, most essentially smashed. He was a very large man, would weigh two hundred and thirty pounds. His first words were, "Why didn't you heave to?" Our skipper replied, "You were gaining so fast I did not think it worth while;

you have a great sailor." This compliment rather pleased Johny Bull; said he, "I have come after my man, where is he?" He was told that he was below, sick. He would like to have him called up. Orders were given for Young to be called, and I came on deck. He looked at me very severely, scrutinized every feature, said, "Do you know that ship?" "I do not, sir; don't think I ever saw her before." "You do," replied he; "you and five others stole my boat and ran away, and carried off our ship's tool." Now don't deny it." "I did not, sir." "Well, did you come on board this ship at Tombez?" "I did sir" "How came you there?" I then repeated the story as the runaway had told it to me. While the conversation was taking place, our crew and the other ship's crew were having a gam together; some of them thought I was the man, as my size corresponded very well, but my voice caused a diversity of opinions among them. I was somewhat amused, as much of their talk was had in my hearing.

Finally turning to our Capt., said he "Captain, is this the man who came on board your ship at Tombez?" He came on board there, on my honor as a man. (It was no lie,—I did several times), "My officers all saw him and recognized him, when he was on the top-gallant masthead; I think we will take him along." "Well," said our Capt., "if the man belongs to your ship you must have him, of course, but you

will have to furnish better proof than you have before
you get him, now that's certain." He again looked
me in the face, asked a few additional questions, then
turning to the Captain, said. "That be d—n for a
yarn, he is not my man ; my officers, don't know as
much as they think they do." He was then asked below to get something to drink, and was not long in
accepting for fear the Capt., might forget about it. I
was dismissed, and went into my bunk again. It was
getting about supper time, both crews were below, and
soon a plenty of rum was passed into the steerage
from the cabin and passed round. They said it was a
good time, but I was getting hungry as well as tired
of my position ; all that I got of it was what I saw
and overheard. Some of the English sailors wanted
me called, being hardly convinced but that I was the
man, but as I was sick they would not disturb
me.

They got to be pretty jolly. Yarns were spun and
songs sung; and the evening was passed in good hum-
or by all on board, — excepting myself, for my mirth
had to be kept under. At eleven o'clock the English
man, with considerable assistance, reached his boat
and they shoved off. I turned out, called the carpenter, and if my clothes didn't look nice ! Dirty water,
grease and iron-rust, beautifully displayed to the very
best advantage. Together the carpenter and myself
supped, he feeling some better than he did a few

hours previous, the shakes having left him when he discovered the Englishman had taken his departure. A laugh went through the ship from stem to stern. while we all felt very much as people do now-a-days when they utter the slang phrase, "Sold again." Frequently afterwards I had to answer to the name of Matthew Young. Next morning the other ship was far away, and soon out of sight entirely. — About a month after fell in with ship Boston, a Nantucket whaler, under the command of a cousin of mine, one Clasby. He visited our ship, and after being on board a while, Capt. Doggett told him the story of the Englishman's experience looking up runaway sailors. He had me called aft, and asked me how I dared to play it on the old fellow in that shape. I told him for two reasons: one was from pity for him, (meaning Young), the other from pity for ourselves, as we were short-handed. He said he should hardly have thought I would have dared to, but it was a pretty slick caper, at any rate. He afterwards saw and conversed with the carpenter about it.

Not a great while from that time, Capt. Clasby fell in with the Englishman, and during a visit to his ship introduced the story as I have told it, by telling the captain that he had 'been on board "the little Yankee ship" (as our vessel was usually called). The English captain said he too was on board of us not a great while before. "Yes," said Clasby, "they served you

a pretty slick caper, didn't they?" " Oh, no, no caper
was served me, it was a mistake ; I thought he had a
man belonging to us, but found the officers to be mistaken. There was no trick however." Said Capt.
Clasby, " It was your man for I saw him and conversed with him. The man you saw belonged to the
ship ; I knew him well, as he was a cousin of mine.
He changed clothes with your man, and while representing him before you, the other man was in the hold."
" Is that so ? " exclaimed the Captain in much surprise. " I have heard before of Yankee tricks, but that
beats all creation." (He might have added, and Johny
Bull in the bargain.) Clasby replied, " It was just as
I tell you ; that boy always was a big rogue, and he
played it pretty well." "Yes, that is a fact ; I often
have heard of Yankee capers, is it possible I have
been made a fool of by one of the same species?
Well, I rather think I have, and, as he is not here to
take a drink, won't you do it for him ? But I want
to live long enough to see him once more." He died
not a great while after ; not, however, from the effect of
the joke played, for no man who was intended for a self-
murderer would ever die from any other cause.

About these times we fared much better for grub.
The bread was headed up, and sweet potatoes were
dealt out ; two middling sized ones or one large one to
a man for each meal. We caught several black-fish, and
had a good store hanging to the main-stay. Some-

tmes had what sailors call "duff," flour and water mixed and boiled in salt water, after being placed in a bag. If a part of it was allowed to get cold it answered the purpose of a whetstone. Now and then the favorite dish of samp, seasoned as before with the fresh meat of worms, was served out. Quite a moderate day, shortly after, all the boats went out after a whale. He ran to windward and before they succeeded in striking him, he was ten miles from the ship. He was an ugly fellow. The captain's boat turned him up and took him in tow. The ship still remaining far off instead of trying to approach the boats, was observed to be acting strangely, sometimes heading on the wind, at another time running free. We hardly knew what to make of it, and some fears were entertained for the safety of the ship keeper in charge. The captain picked a crew of his best men and pulled for the vessel, boarding which, he found things not exactly as he would have liked. In a few hours the boats with the whale reached the ship, and early next morning all hands were engaged cutting in, trying out and stowing down. He ·made us fifty barrels. We said to the captain that it was unsafe to leave the ship as we had done previously; we thought it as well to put some other person in charge. He replied that it was his intention to select a new ship-keeper, and calling me aft told me I was needed in that capacity. I told him that was not what I shipped for, nor did I desire the position. "It is your duty to do anything that is for the interest of the voyage," he replied. In answer to this, told him I was fearful of not being able to suit him, that he had better se ject some other person. "No," said he, "you may keep the ship." I then asked if I was not entitled to a ship-keeper's lay? "Certainly you are, and you shall have it." "Well, sir, I would like to have it in writing, for something to show will be required in settling the voyage." He showed some little anger, and asked me if his word was not to be taken. I replied, "It is to be hoped sir, that it may be good But there is no disputing what is shown in black and white." He gave me no writing, but the position was accepted on his promise to do so, which he failed to fulfil. Soon a good opportunity was offered for showing my abilities in my new cast of character. A large whale had been raised, all the boats were in pursuit; when they struck, were well to windward of the ship. With the assistance of a boy twelve years of age, the ship had to be work-ed against the wind, and before they succeeded in fetching the whale to, he had run still further off. The ship was anciently rigged, every rope of hemp, mostly stiffened with tar, and consequently exceeding clumsy. 1 hauled ropes, braces, sheets and tacks, till from my eyes flashed streams of fire as protract-ed as herring-sticks. At last got the ship up, hove a back, and the whale was taken alongside. When the captain came on board, he complimented me in unmeasured terms; perfectly satisfied with my first attempt at ship-keeping. Well he might have been, thought I. We cut the whale in, and he stowed down forty barrels.

Our water casks getting low, concluded to put away for Tombez once more. We had a good spell of quiet on board, but little growling, pleasant weather, and short passage Dropped anchor off bar, soon filled our casks and replenished the wood pile. Mr. Godfrey, a townsman of ours, was quite sick below. Capt. D.· ordered me to go down and pass up everything which belonged to Mr. G., as he was intending to put him on shore I told him that I did not care to comply with his request, when he gave the order to another who attended to it. The captain picked out six of us, who he said were afflicted with the scurvy, saying that he had made arrangements with a planter to fresh provision us on his plantation in the interior, for a while. I told im that no indication of that complaint was on my body, nor in my system, but the boat was lowered and for the plantation we started. Had a good time eating country produce for four days. On the morning of the fifth day our boat landed for us, the one in charge informing us· that the ship was soon to leave port. Inquiries being made for Mr. G., were told that the other boat had gone to the village for him. When we reached the ship the other boats were there, and had not been to the village for the sick man. Capt. Daggett and Mathew Young, during our temporary absence, had been having a little bit of a row in relation to the immoderate use of corn served out to the hogs about deck (I allude to the four legged ones). The captain told him he feed them too high, to which accusation he pleaded not guilty, and enforced his words by the use of some considered (in cabin circles) rather insulting. It finally resulted in Young's getting his ribs stove in by an unlucky hoist given him by our not over very stiff-jointed Captain. This was in the afternoon. Next morning a little Drogar anchored near us, just in from down the coast. Our mate sung out, "Man the boat," calling Young to get in with the others. We pulled off and boarded the craft ; found plenty of wine and *aguardiente* on board, which was passed around quite freely. Directly looking toward the ship, saw that she was getting under way. Mate cried out, "Man the boat," and we jumped in and shoved off. Soon noticed that Young was missing, but the mate said no matter, we could send a boat for him. The ship was headed out to sea, all sail on her ; we caught up, and took in the boats. Mr. Godfrey and Matthew Young were left behind. The place was soon lost to our view and I have never seen it since, nor do I expect to.

None of us expected to ever see Godfrey again, but we' did ; for when we arrived home at the end of the voyage, he had reached there in advance of us.

We soon arrived on whale ground, two hands short er than we were before entering port. Had been cruising only a few days, when a large ship was seen bearing down towards us. She came close aboard, ounded to under our lee, and hove aback. We soon ecognized her as the same formerly commanded by the old Englishman, who we afterwards learned had died, and the command devolved upon his former mate, who manned his boat and boarded us. Almost the first words he uttered were, "Where's our man?" He was informed that we left him on shore at Tombez. The statement was received with some doubt. He said, "I don't want him, I wouldn't have him on board the ship if I could as well as not, but would like to talk with him." "He is not here, for certain." "Well," said he, "then allow me to see the person who represented him in such a rascally manner, I had the whole story from Captain Clasby. I was called aft, and of all the mad men I ever saw, the Old Man was the madest. When I was introduced by our captain as the chap he inquired for, I looked him in the face, hardly able to restrain my laughter. Said I, "How do you do, sir?" He replied, "You are the fellow who so deceived Capt. Graham, are you? How dared you do it? Had you known him as well

as I did, you would hardly have considered it safe."
" Well sir," I replied, I should not think so trifling
an incident worth speaking of." He replied that it
was pretty well done none but a Yankee would have
thought of it. "I will give you the credit of carrying
out a good joke in pretty nice shape, and if you are
as good a sailor as you are a Yankee trickster and
friend to Matthew Young, the runaway English tar,
you must be a valuable man." Upon inquiring particularly about Capt. Graham, were told he died of
delirium tremens. He was a most inveterate drinker
and the verdict rendered in his case was, "Rum did
it." We parted company with the ship soon after,
and saw her no more during the voyage.

The next day raised another large whale. As before
I was left in charge of the ship, all the boats in pursuit, and the whale far to windward. The Capt. got
fast, but lost a good chance to lance him, by allowing
his boatsteerer to practice the profession of bleeding;
the business being new to him, he failed to do much
execution. The whale sounded, took out all the line
in the boat, when the second Mate's boat came up,
and Mr. Arcy, the boat header, bent on another one
He still sank deeper, taking a good part of the second
line. Presently began to haul line and gradually he
arose to near the surface of the water. The Capt
seeing Mr. A. getting ready to lance, told him not t
kill that whale, for he wanted Mr. Boatsteerer Norto

to kill him. (Here let me remark, boatsteerers on board the old ship Appollo were always addressed as "Mr."). Mr. A. replied, "If the whale comes up near to me, I will throw a lance into him, if some one comes out of the grave to forbid it." He did come up all right, and all he had to do was to start the claret on him, which he did; turned him up in less time than required to tell it. When the Old Man saw the blood flying, he sang out, "Well done, my good lad; you have done it nicely." "Yes," said Mr. A., "but if I hadn't killed him, Tophet would not have been enough for me, according to your views." My best endeavors were used in getting the ship conven- ient to the boats. Got the whale cut in, which stowed us down between fifty and sixty barrels. We did not pretend, in those early years of whaling, to make any account of the teeth, only saving them occasionally for the purpose of "scrimshawning," as sailors term the making of fancy articles from the parts of the whale. After this, business was dull for some months, but an ncident occured in a few days which served to give a little variety to the monotony of sea life.

The day was moderate; hardly a ripple disturbed the broad expense of water which surrounded us. The lookout, at the fore-top-gallant mast-head, saw something in the distance making for the ship. Some curiosity was manifested, until from its near approach it was discovered to be one of the larger species of turtle,

Mr. Norton immediately ordered the Captain's boat cleared away for lowering; a number jumped in and. chase was given him. As they pulled up behind, Norton stood ready with the boat-hook, intending to enter it into the jaw, or forward of the fore flipper. Made the attempt, but as the skin was unyielding and the hook rather dull, missed his aim, which only had the effect of waking him up from the little nap he was quite innocently enjoying. He dove under water about ten or a dozen feet. Mr Norton saw where he was, saying, "Mr. Turtle, you are not to give us the slip quite as easy as you imagine," slat his hat into the bottom of the boat, overboard, and under after him. Grabbed him aft, bearing down pointed him upward. The old turtle came up near the boat under full pressure, when he was secured and safely lodged on board. Do not know how he liked boat-sailing, but probably he had never before enjoyed such a luxury. The turtle was after the Hawkbill species, his mouth and head very much resembling the bird of that name. He weighed two hundred pounds. It was a foolish experiment for a man to try ; had the animal been disposed to draw his hind flippers up, Mr. Norton could never have been extricated himself, and consequently must have been lost beyond the hope of recovery. I imagine that was the first, and probably the last time that Mr Norton ever became so attached to one of those naturally ugly quadrapeds.

Our cruising for whales was attended with but little success, though one was taken occasionally. When the boats left early in the morning, no cooking was done for the day; but if the "Doctor" had time to put a dinner on to cook, I was usually attended to its completion in his absence. About this time our Skipper thought he would put away for Paiti (a seaport of Peru). Had to beat against trade winds, and in about ten days made the land. Standing into a bay, saw a curious looking craft coming out; soon coming together, it proved to be what was termed a "Catamaran," constructed of fourteen logs, thirty-five feet in length, secured by trenails. It was very light wood, the large ends were aft, each log sharpened in front like a wedge, a platform four feet high a little abaft the centre with a thatched house upon it, the water passing over the logs and under the house. On boarding her, ascertained that she had a cargo of fruit and quite a number of passengers. Were informed that they were bound to Paiti also, and her commander said he would keep our company. The idea seemed so ridiculous that we laughed, for we had considered our ship a very superior sailing craft. We purchased some fruits.

The Catamaran had two masts, on each of which was a large square sail made of grass mats. We were told that we were two miles to leeward of P. Stood out of the bay in company, sharp hauled on the

wind. We noticed that the man who was steering
our fancy neighbor stood knee deep in the water.
Tacked several times. but no great difference was discovered in the sailing qualities of either vessel. All
day we kept within a quarter of a mile of each other;
she held us very good play, her centre-board holding
her up to the wind. Just at night a smart breeze
sprang up. We reefed but one topsail at a time, keeping our headway. The other lowered both sails at
once, and was a great while taking in the reefs, and
by that means she got some distance to leeward of
us. Soon the darkness hid her from our view, and
we have not seen her since. We worked along until
we judged ourselves all right to go in by daylight;
stood off shore under short sail, with orders to keep
that course until two o'clock, then to tack and run in.
It was my trick at the wheel. Just before the hour
of two the Captain and mate came on deck, the captain saying he had altered his mind and should not
enter Paiti, for fear of detention if there was trouble
between the Patriots and Loyalists. " I think," said
he, " we had better go to the Gallipagos Islands ; there
we can get some terrapin if nothing else." The charts
were soon spread on the cabin table, the course traced
and distance estimated down to the Islands, and for
them the ship was headed. ·

Light winds prevailed and our progress was very
slow. Took no oil on the passage. After many days

reached Charles Island, where we fell in with two
Englishman whalers and a Nantucketer. We came to
anchor close by them, and everything being secure went
on shore after terrapin. Went far into the interior
over to Black Beach, so called from its cinderry
appearance. Trees called cabbage wood and prickly
pears were scattered here and there; only one spring
of water was found, and that on the extreme south end.
We succeeded in taking a good lot of terrapin, usually
selecting those most convenient to carry on our backs,
the usual way of transporting them.

Here we remained about one week, occupying ourselves daily in the same manner Frequently it required some time to enable us to find the sized ones
best suited to our ideas ; they were all the way from
as large as a silver dollar to the size of a Henry Clay
cook stove. Some were so large that they could easily travel with four good-sized men on their backs.
Their chief article of diet when on land is the cab-
bage-tree leaves, which are broken down by the force
of the winds; but sometimes when no high winds lay
their food on the ground for them, a large number
will congregate, and with one accord gnaw into the
bark of these trees, till, coming to the pith which is
soft and tender, the tree falls before them. The trees
grow to the size of half-barrel. I have often taken
them from their work and pointed them in another
direction, but if allowed they will return to complete

their job, never leaving it until it is completed.
Though they appear to enjoy eating as well as other
animals, yet they will live and thrive on ship-board
for months or more, with ·nothing on which to sub-
sist.

Three hundred were put on board our ship, stowed
between decks or anywhere out of the way. They
were a strange kind of birds; did not seem to care
whether they stood on their head or heels. Their
meat was most excellent; usually made it into stifles
and soups. They were so fat that half a bucket full
of grease could be taken from their upper shell when
butchered. The fat was sometimes used to shorten
those favorite· " duffs " previously alluded to.

More or less gamming was attended to, from one
ship to another; on one of these occasions, Capt.
Coffin of the Nantucket ship, told us one of his men, an
Indian from Gray Head, had been missing for some
days; did not know but that some accident had be-
fallen him. He was nowhere to be found, and as he
was going down to Tee Bay, wished us, if he turned
up, to bring him along with us when we came down.
It was our intention to leave in a day or two.
On the night previous to our leaving, our mate ordered the boat manned ; said he was going to visit the
English ship. I started to get into the boat with
others belonging to her, when the mate told me it
was the the captain's orders that I should remain by

the ship. I did not believe it, however, and while the mate went to the cabin for something he had left, I jumped into her and hid myself under some old jackets in the bow. The boat went alongside the ship, all hands including myself scrabbled up, it was quite dark, and I escaped the notice of the mate. I went into the forecastle, and there saw the Gay Head Indian whom I recognized from the Nantucket kersey of• which his clothing was composed. He was very composedly taking his supper. Looking him in the face, said I, "Hallo, Gay Head, how came you here?" He replied, "1 belong to this ship." "Well," said I, "you have belonged to her only one day." He left in disgust, and I saw him no more for the night.

Soon after it was "man the boat;" the mate catching sight of me said, "How the d—l came you here?" In reply told him that he brought me." "Did you come off in the boat? I· did not see you." " I did, sir, but didn't intend you should see me; I was covered up in the bow of the boat. It passed off and nothing more was said about it. The next morning, preparations being made to go out, I asked the captain if he wasn't going to take Capt. Coffin's Gay Header to him? He replied, if he knew where he was should do so. " Well," said I, " he is on· board the English ship ; I saw him and conversed with him when on board the ship last night." As no comments were made regarding my visiting the ship, it satisfied me

that the mate lied to me the night before. The object
he had in view I never learned. The boat was lowered,
and I was ordered to accompany the crew for a visit
to the ship. Upon reaching her the captain was informed that we had come after Capt. Coffin's runaway
sailor. He replied that he knew nothing about him,
he was not on board his ship that he knew of. I was
then asked if I didn't see him in the forecastle the
last night? replied that I did, and going down found
him still there. He was ordered up, and we took him
aboard with us.; he was rather sulky, didn't wish to
go. He was told that it was Capt. Coffin's wish for
us to bring him to his ship, and we intended to do
so.

When we got down, set our signals for Coffin to
board us. The mate came and took him into his boat;
when they shoved off, the Indian took an oar as if to
assist in rowing but instead darted it through the
planks of the bow, making a hole in her which required
stuffing with old rags to prevent sinking. The mate
told him he would sweaten him, and no doubt he did.
It was not characteristic of the race to be very evil-
minded; this case was an exception rather than an
example of the general rule. Perhaps no class of
people on the globe have won a fairer reputation for
bravery and seamanship or the enviable qualities of
superior whalemen. No better recommendation was
required by those engaged in the whaling interest,

than to be assured that an individual belonged to the
Gay Head tribe, or was the descendent of such

The full-blooded of that race have become almost
extinct. Deacon Johnson, an old and much respected
Baptist veteran, is I believe, the only living represen-
tative.

The terrapin we had taken were stowed in different
parts of the ship, some among the casks between decks,
some on deck ; it mattered little to us, and apparently
less to them, what their accomodations were, so long
as they kept out from under foot. With the food they
afforded and that of the blackfish constantly on hand,
we fared quite sumptuously.

We continued our cruising in company with the
ships, with but little success for some time, and the
captain thought best to return to his old whale ground.
Headed her off that way, always maintaining a lookout
at masthead. Got pretty well back. At this time the
carpenter Mr. B. Smith, was sick and unable to go in
the boats. It was my lookout ; was at the main top
gallant head, discovered a very large spout of a sperm
whale along way to leeward. Sang out, "There she
blows ! a sperm whale of the beam ! " The wind was
light, kept off for him. The whale went down and
stayed down an hour, then spouted again and started
to leeward ; kept up one hour, by the glass. Captain
said he must be a large fellow. Were going so slowly,
concluded to chase with the boats. All three boats

were lowered and off after him. I was left with the
sick man, who was just able to walk ; had to sit down
to steer. Well for us that the whale was so far to leeward, it was my intention to keep him so as long as
possible. Didn't run down very fast for fear he would
turn to windward. I went aloft with the glass, and
judged that the whale was about three miles away.;
very soon saw white water, and concluded they were
fast, which was the case. About the same time I observed an ugly looking squall rising to the windward,
and I knew if sail was not shortened, before it shut us
in from the boats, they would cut from and loose the
whale. •

I hurried down, set the bearings of the whale by the
compass, and told the sick man we must contrive to
rake in the light sails. First the mizzen, then the
fore and main top gallant sails were taken in. Hauled
the foresail up snug, then slewed the ship broadside
to the boats that it might be seen that it was un-
necessary for them to cut, that sail had already been
shortened ready for a squall. It was observed just in
time to prevent them from cutting. The squall struck,
but not so heavy as was anticipated, though she
groaned for a while. After it passed, headed her for
the boats. The whale had acted pretty ugly, and was
still spouting thick blood ; one boat was badly stove,
but pretty soon the whale was dead.

Run the ship down and hove her aback, a line was

ran to the ship, and the whale taken alongside quite late in the day. The captain was much pleased with our management on board the ship, said he couldn't have done better himself, adding. "You saved the whale for us." Cut him in the next day, that is, what the sharks didn't carry off; we stowed down ninety barrels, and probably ten or fifteen barrels was pilfered by the sharks, many of whom during the night became the victims of our displeasure, for we disliked to feed them on such expensive food and gave them cold iron instead.

Our foretopsail now beginning to look pretty black on account of places worn thin, a man was sent aloft to remedy the evil by making them blacker, by giving them a coat of tar; and entirely original method of mending old sails. Several times this was resorted to, and by the time our voyage was accomplished it had a most singular appearance. Had used the foresail for the whole voyage. Whales were scarce after this time, and it was judged best to try our luck on the inshore ground; accordingly put her away for the coast. Our cook (or "doctor," as he was usually called), used to parboil a sufficient quantity of terrapin over night for next morning's breakfast, when not obliged to be in the boats. At this time had some already prepared. Quite often in his absence I would do it for him, during my deck watch.

The sweet potatoes had now become so scarce they

were only served up in the cabin, but during the day a boatsteerer had contrived to hook a bucket full. It was our watch from eight o'clock to twelve. Our caboose stood forward against the bowsprit bitts, the forecastle gangway being on the port bow. The boat-steerer told me he wanted the potatoes boiled. I told him that as we were heading for the land, the old man would be around and it had better be put off for another time.

It was a pleasant night; I went below and took a little nap on my chest. Presently one of the watch came down and woke me, saying, "come on deck, we have a good fire in the galley, and the potatoes are boiling and nearly done, but the captain is in the smoke and we dare not take 'em out. What had we better do?" I replied, "'Tis a mess of your own cooking, I'm sure I don't know what to prescribe." Just at this time the captain growled out, "What is all this fire doing here?" With a lie already on the end of my tongue I replied, "We have tarrapin on parboiling." "Who has the care of it?" he asked "I have, sir," I replied. "Well, come along and at-tend to it then." "There is a good fire, sir." "Yes, I see there is enough to roast a bullock; throw some water on it, you don't need so much." Glad of the opportunity of shedding less light on the subject, soon extinguished the flames to his satisfaction, and no less to our own.

The rest of the watch were well aft, hoping he would come to. them. " Now," said he to me," go aloft and see if any land is in sight." I started up the weather-rigging (he was on the lee-side of the vessel, reached the foreyard, and perceiving him going toward the men aft, I crossed over and came down the lee side, dodged into the galley, and before you could say Jack Robinson relieved the coppers of the potatoes, but found the captain coming forward again. Not having time to remove them without his knowledge, slid the door too as far as it would slide. He appeared to be heading for the galley : said I, " I think, sir, the land is in sight." " Gosh souls ! where away ? said he. I pointed off the lee bow to a heavy bank in the horizon. " Come this way, lads," he ordered, " and tell me what you make of this " As quick as his attention was directed toward what I very well knew was only a cloud, I started into the forecastle with the potatoes in a little less than no time. My next manœuvre was to place the kid of parboiled terrapin where he could not fail to see it, if his attention was given in that direction,

It being decided not land, the captain wheeled round and asked, " Isn't that terrapin done yet ? " Said I, " Yes sir, here it is in the kid ; " but he didn't feel of it, and I was glad he did not, for its coldness would have betrayed me. " Well, out with the fire then ; we have no wood to throw away," he added, and went

aft. It was now nearly time for the next watch to be
called. The old darky cook slept in the forecastle
alone, and when he slept he did it very soundly. I
attempted to make him understand how things were in
regard to potatoes, told him if the old man questioned ·
him, to let him think I had been assisting him with
the terrapin, &c. He appeared to be drowsey, did not
seem to comprehend the situation, and in order to
arouse his faculties I sawed his legs across the edge
of the berth boards till he began to swear, when I
knew he was awake. I told him where the terrapin
were stowed, but he of course was to know nothing
but terrapin if any enquiries were made, and promised
him if he carried it out slick he should have the next
glass of grog that was served out to me. I knew this
would make it a sure pop with him, if anything could.

The next morning the cook went into the hold for
wood ; had thrown quite a pile up on deck, when the
captain ordered him aft. He went, said the captain,
" Such work as this won't do, cook." What work
asked he, " Well," said the captain, " it takes half
the night to prepare terrapin for breakfast." The cook
said it couldn't be helped ; he didn't always have time,
and so got others to help with it. " Who had the
care last night?" " Ripley," replied the cook.
" What ! do you trust that fellow with the fire at night?"
"Yes sir ; he said he would have a good lookout, and
do it all right." "I should say he was as good as

his word ; he had a roarer. I'm afraid he will burn us all up yet, he's all over the ship in an hour ; you must try to attend to it yourself in the future." The cook replied that he always had when he could. That wound up the affair except eating the potatoes which relished remarkably well, tasting all the better for the trouble taken in securing them. The captain turning to the pile of wood said, "Look here cookey, you know we are getting short of wood ; you must heave part of that into the hold again. Here Edmund, (addressing his son), go below and get a glass of grog for the cook." The wood-pile diminished rapidly, and so did the grog shortly after.

The boy had been in the habit of bringing liquor into the steerage for the cooper and carpenter, both having through life been accustomed to it. The captain thought it too bad for them to be denied it now, when it was almost second nature to them. On one occasion of the boy's "spiritual" visit, in fun I remarked that I wished I was a cooper, carpenter, or some other mechanical devil, that I might have a little once in a while. The boy left, but soon returned and said, " Ripley, father wants you in the cabin." What is the matter now ? thought I. What I had done of a serious nature to offend, I was unable to conjecture ; told the boy when they had done their dinner in the cabin, I would come and see him. He carried my reply and immediately returned, saying, " Father wants

you now, Ripley." This time I went, and as I approached the table Capt. Daggett asked me if I was a
cooper? "No, sir," said I. "Are you a carpenter?'
"No, sir; but I can make a box that will hold sweet
potatoes." "Goshsouls!" he exclaimed, (a favorite
expression of his). "Well Ripley," said he, "repeat
what you said to the boy when he brought the grog
into the steerage." Said I, "there was no harm intended, sir; having often seen the boy on his mission,
I uttered the expression referred to." The bottle was
on the table, which, with a tumbler, he shoved over
to me, saying. "Now take a good drink yourself;
knowing how much you have knocked around the world,
I ought to have considered you in connection with the
others. But help yourself and don't be afraid of it."
Not knowing its contents, I replied that to drink after
him was manners. A moderate drink was poured out
which I drank, while he insisted that as there was a
plenty of it I must not slight it. I remarked that a
little suited me best. "In the future," said the captain, "when the cooper and carpenter have their grog,
yours will be sent also; but as to the boys, they are
better without it. He was true to his word, but it
didn't often occur, and so my constitution was not
injured by excessive indulgence.

About this time, fearful that our skipper would not
know the circumstances of the potatoe-cooking, I told
the story as it was, in the presence of a person who

had won the reputation of being a mail-carrier on board the ship. The same day the captain came to me and said : " Ripley, I understand you are a good hand to boil potatoes in the night." I replied that I was, if while so doing I could lead him to suppose the land was in sight. " Yes," said he, " that was all that saved your bacon ; it was a nice caper, and I will give you credit for it." " Well," said I, " suppose you had found it out at the time ?" He replied that it would have gone hard with me.

Most every day more or less patches of tar were made on the foretopsail. Still we cruised for whales sometimes for weeks without seeing a spout, and then raise a whale only to chase the whole day without getting him A week later, no land in sight, saw a large school of sperm whales going to windward very fast. Lowered all the boats ; one boat got fast to a little fellow, the others kept on in the hope of catching up with the others, but gave it up, and returned to assist in towing the other whale now dead. He had acted quite strangely before the thick blood was fetched, turning round and round. On examining him, was found to be blind in one eye, and his object in turning to the right was to bring his left to bear upon the boat ; which, as the boat turned with his movement, he was unable to do, and the difficulty under which he labored was not obviated.

The whale was taken to the ship, making only

thirty-five barrels. Saw no more chances for ten days or a fortnight. A few more patches of tar were added to the topsail. Not long after saw a large school of fine seal, asleep on the water. One boat put off in pursuit, paddling up to leeward that they might not scent their pursuers Killed one with the spade or lance; he was about as large as the body of a small horse; hoisted him in and hauled him into the lee waist. One of the officers requested me to skin him, I went at it, while the most of the crew acted as spectators. Was at work about the head, and lifting the skin opened his mouth, and displayed two jaws of very black teeth. The captain, wishing for a good sight; said, " Ripely, open his mouth again," I did so, when the captain exclaimed as usual, " Goslisouls! what do you suppose ails the critter?" I replied that without any doubt he had eaten so much salt meat it had brought on the scurvy, and that must be the cause of his teeth being so black. He made no more comments and walked aft. The cooper said it was a wonder I didn't get my brains knocked out, answering the captain that way. I told him it was no easy matter to knock out brains where there was a general scarcity of them. The skin of the seal was used to cover chafed parts of the rigging, the blubber was tried out and found to yield an excellent oil. The balance was given to the sharks. We had frequently taken seal but none so large.

As the terrapin had become nearly exhausted, having given many to other ships, blackfish was chiefly served out to us for meat.

The bright waist looking rather tarnished, thought best to give it a coat of paint, for which, from the lack of anything better, we took porpoise oil mixed with tar, and soot from the cooks funnel, which looked very well when first put on, but during the night the sea was rough, and before morning the paint was washed off, leaving it in a still worse condition than before. That was all the painting done for the voyage. Were now working up the coast toward Cape Horn. Saw one lone sperm whale; he was moving very slow, put after him with two boats and soon fastened and killed him. A good reason was manifest why he was so moderate in his movements. His tail was nearly rotted off, and his body was covered with eruptions; was a sight to behold. He was as large as a fifty barrel whale, but we only got twenty. This was the last sperm whale taken during the voyage, making eight hundred and eight barrels altogether. As the prospect now looked bad for getting more, concluded to put away for the Brazil Banks, in quest of right whale.

With a fair wind and plenty of it, soon got around the cape ; three days we scud under a reefed topsail alone. Saw a number of ships but spoke none. Occasionally a whale was seen, but as it was quite rugged did not put the boats out. In due time arrived at the banks; found whales to be quite numerous; one day lowered two boats, the rugged weather requiring a boat's crew to remain on board the ship. They struck, but not being acquainted with right whaling, he was not secured. Not long after it was "lower away" again; managed to get one this time, a very large fellow. It was cold and rough whaling, and it didn't take us long to get disgusted with it. We well knew the oil was hardly worth boiling out, and frequently would chase a long time, strike and part our lines, or the whale would sink. Luck seemed to be against us; we were about disheartened, and wished to leave the business.

Just after taking another whale, it began to blow; we had to take in the fore and mizzen topsails and close reef the main. When we came to furl the fore topsail, it required all hands and took an hour to roll it up. The thick patches of tar, and it being extremely cold, it was like handling a side of sole leather. The roll was as large as a four barrel cask.

Shortly after had pleasant weather again. Saw whales quite often; killed and sank half a dozen; only saved one, for our lines were getting very rotten. A few days after we were again compelled to reef as fast as we could. We were laying on the starboard tack; it was my watch on deck, and the sea was getting very rough. She fetched a deep roll to leeward, struck the waist boat on the water, and unhooked the forward tackle, partially filling her with water. The gripes were parted, and when the ship rolled to windward, the boat struck her with great force and considerable racket. We were in hopes she would break away and clear herself from the ship, for fear the captain might be disturbed; but as we concluded to get her in, called all hands and got her in on deck. The officers went below. On account of the roughness, the cabin lamp was left on the floor, burning dimly. The mate undertook to increase the flame by picking up the wick, neither he nor the captain meanwhile being in the best of humor. The captain angrily asked him what he was trying to do; Said he, "I am trying to coax this lamp to burn; your d—d lazy boy hasn't trimmed it to-night." By that he clenched the mate, but by some means tumbled against a chest, which knocked from his cheek a piece of skin as large as a silver quarter of a dollar. They had quite a squabble, but I did not see who came off best, nor did I much care.

Next day it was rugged, no whales in sight; the captain and mate were on deck. All hands were called aft, and the captain addressing the crew said, "Do you see my face? Mr. Luce struck me last night." Mr. Luce denied the assertion, said that the scar was made by the captain falling against the corner of a chest. To which the captain replied, "Mr. Luce, you

are no longer an officer on board this ship, I break
you, and it is my orders that hereafter the crew do
not regard your commands, neither men nor boys,
under penalty of having their voyage stopped when we
get home." The crew all liked Mr. Luce, and preferred him for mate ; did not know whom he would
appoint, and it was very evident that a general dis-
satisfaction existed with the present arrangement, by
the lit le squads of men scattered here and there about
the vessel, in earnest conversation. The captain perceived this to be the case, and calling the cooper
one side asked him to inform him just how things were
in relation to it, said he, " Are the fellows going to
mutiny and take the ship ?" " Well," siad the cooper,
" they don't like your proceedings, are not satisfied
with your breaking the mate, they want no other one
to take his place, and will not stand it." Said the
captain, " I have forbidden all hands obeying him, I
dislike to take back my words, but if he will make
acknowledgment and take his place like a man, they
may obey him as heretofore." We asked him to take
the place of mate on . the conditions named. He replied he would see him d——d first before he would
acknowledge ; he had nothing to acknowledge to him
for. He took his place, and things went on as before.

All hands still sicker of whaling than ever, concluded
the best move next made would be toward home.

Headed her that way; had a good run, with fair winds. Made the coast of North America first off Montoguo Point. We took no pilot, as one of the boatsteerers used to follow the business, and was familar with the coast. He was given charge. When we reached the flats opposite the harbor of Edgartown, a lot of boats came to us, they having heard of our approach. The captain jumped into one of the sailboats and went on shore. The wind being now ahead, we had to beat into the harbor, and the pilot allowing his attention to be given too much to visitors, the first thing we knew the ship fetched up on the northeast end of Chappaquiddic, on Stony Point, Cape Pogue.

It was now near night, and we sent up town for a smack. Sent down the three top-gallant masts, and in the evening, the vessel arriving, got out a large anchor with a long scope of cable. At high water hove her off and ran up to Dea. Mayhew's wharf. Almost the first man we saw was Mr. Godfrey, whom we supposed long since dead and buried in Tombez. Left penniless as he was in a foreign country, he had managed to pick his way from one land to another, swimming rivers penetrating forests, sometimes getting a short lift from one conveyance by land, at another by water; at last arriving before us. He was a good navigator, and this must have done him good service.

We tied her up, furled the sails, and if any one

wished to see a rough looking vessel, they had only to visit Mayhew's wharf to do so.

The oil turned out 1011 barrels, which was sold at the rate of thirty-eight cents per gallon for the sperm, and twenty-two for the right whale. My wages after settling the voyage amounted to seven dollars ·per month; was absent twenty-two months, and I was perfectly satisfied that I had seen all the experience I desired in the whaling business. My outfit cost me thirty dollars, and on my return. brought back in good condition twenty dollars worth. This ship afterwards made two quite successful voyages sperm whaling, and was finally condemned and hauled into the shore, below the residence of her chief owner. Here for many years her hulk lay, a fitting memento of the early enterprise of those who sent her out. Recently the naked timbers, over which the tide ebbed and flowed twice in twenty-four hours for so many years, were removed for the sake of the copper fastenings; but a knee, termed the dead wood, which was a part of the stern work, may yet be seen on the premises belonging to the town poorhouse, and although it connot be less than eighty-five years old, no sign of decay is visible upon it. This should, and doubtless will be, preserved by some of our enterprising citizens as a relic of the first vessel engaged in this interest by our townspeople, as well as a memorial perpetuating the names of those who performed the voyage, two of whom only survive, viz; Capt. G. A. Baylies, and the subject of this narrative.

CHAPTER XIX.

AFTER remaining at home a few weeks, spending my leisure time in the society of my friends, finding that my long absence had not diminished the interest I had felt in them in times past. From intimations received from parties concerned, in regard to lawsuits about to be instituted between different parties who were on board the old Appollo, thought to avoid appearing as evidence by making a voyage south.

Shipped on board a coaster called the Native. We proceeded to Boston, took in a load of salt for Gloucester, delivered it without any particular incident attending us, with the single exception of a little bit of romance with which I was connected. We were lying alongside the wharf, just as the sun was going down on a Sunday evening. A young man in company with two young ladies came to the vessel, and asked me for the use of our boat to take a little moonlight excursion. I told him if he would moor the boat under the bow as he found her, I had no objection to his using her. He took the girls into the boat and started down the harbor.

172

Soon after dark I turned in; lay a spell but was very restless; thought all the mosquitoes and flies in creation were about me. I turned out and went upon deck to get some fresh air, as it was warm. Took a seat on the quarter-deck; soon perceived the boat was returning and near at hand. The young man laid the oars down, and took hold of one of his companions, said, " Now, Mary Ann, I'm going to dip you." " Oh," said she, " don't James; these are my best clothes! " He replied, " I don't care, overboard you go," and pushed her headlong into the water. She turned and clutched the gunwale of the boat. "Ah," said he, "that wont do; you are going all under; a Baptist shall be made of you." " Well, then, please let me remove my combs," which being done, he unclasped her hands and pushed her entirely from sight.

I had been observing the movements, unseen by them, and could not determine what to think about it. When he was ready he hauled her in, and sculled the boat to the bows of the vessel, and darted the oar upon the wharf. The lady who was dry landed in safety, although the boat was not secured by her warp; while the other lady, in attempting unaided to gain the wharf, reached it with her hands, but in the act shoved the boat off, so that before she could get out or recover her position again, went plump into the water. She sank out of sight; the other lady, who was her sister, screamed out, " Mary Ann is drowning! " Soon the drowning girl rose to the surface, raised one arm, screached in agony, and disappeared again; while her male companion bewildered and half drunk, stood quite motionless and stupefied. Said I, "jump and catch that woman, or she will never rise again." Thus aroused, over he went, caught her, and held her head out of the water.

With a long pull I reached the boat, pulled it in, jumped into it and went to rescue them; first pulled in the girl, afterwards got the man in. By this time a dozen or more, who had heard the cries of the sinking girl, had appeared in their sleeping apparel to witness the scene.

Sent the excursion party home, telling them I would take care of the boat. I never saw them after, but learned that they were the daughters of a widow lady, one of whom was receiving the attentions of their brutal companion. He was an intemperate fellow, and this little circumstance ended the courtship.

Our craft returned to Boston, took in an assorted cargo for New York, where we arrived in safety and discharged it all right. Loaded with corn and flour for Boston. Contrasting our present manner of living with whalemen's fare, we considered ourselves in clover. Fair winds prevailing, got along nicely; sometimes the tide or wind heading us, we would run into Edgartown for a harbor, stopping a day or a night, giving me the opportunity of going out on the Great Plain, where a

THE MARRIAGE   Page 175.

certain young lady would receive my friendly visits quite naturally by this time.

On arriving at Boston, a cargo of plaster awaiting our trasportation, a gang of Irishmen very vigorously discharged our grain, by the aid of a spiritual manifestation which they had furnished very liberally, with the promise of remuncration in proportion to their diligence. It was lively work until the cargo was stored. Next day loaded for Richmond, Va., sailing the following day. Soon arrived, finding the weather so extremely hot could hardly breathe. Took in a load of sea coal for Albany, arrived and discharged, took in grain again for the Boston market, and continued making these trips until sometime in November, when the vessel was laid up and all hands discharged. We returned to the Vineyard, as usual glad to get home, and perhaps a little more so.

My mind was now occupied with a very important circumstance, the anticipation of which I had treasured for five years past. Only a few days more, and I hoped to realizé the consumation of all my cherished plans. The young lady, (whom I have already introduced to you), would be twenty-seven on Christmas and preferring to be married before reaching that age, the wedding was appointed to take place at the residence of the bride's father, on the afternoon of Dec. 24th, 1818. On that occasion we received the cordial greeting of many dear friends, not forgetful of course

of good old Aunt Debby. As their was no lack in the
provision made for the entertainment, it was considered
a gay and festive time. ˙ As the fashions of olden times
warranted and rather expected, a generous supply of
cake and wines were furnished, without any regard to
anything but the wishes of our guests.

All appeared to enjoy the occasion. The merry laugh
passed around, and jokes were indulged in until, at a
reasonable hour, with the congratulations of our friends
stamped upon our united hearts, we saw them take
their leave.

Merry Christmas was celebrated by the second edition
of our wedding party, given at my mother's, much
after the fashion of the previous day, leaving out the
marriage ceremony, which did not require repeating,
as Parson Thaxter had a way of doing such jobs that
it never, or rarely, happened that it had to be performed the second time to make it strong. After our
union, until the first of February remained with my new
bride. The weather was as mild as May, and it was
thought Winter had broken. On the first of February,
in Company with Capt. Ripley, started for Boston, by
crossing the sound and then proceeding by the route
overland. He was to take charge of the vessel we
laid up in the fall, and I had agreed to go his mate.
Reached Boston the next night. A heavy gale with a
regular northeast snow storm blocked up our doing
anything for a number of days, but tried to make our-

selves as comfortable as possible at the hotel where we
got entertainment. As the weather became settled and
the snow so leveled we could get about, went on board.
We took in a cargo of new rum and bar iron, also a
few passengers, — one lady and a number of gentlemen,
and started.

We got down to Georges Island; the wind coming
out to the Eastward, and it begining to snow, we came
to anchor under the lee of the island. It was a very
tough storm. We lay four or five days, when, the
wind coming fair, we had a good run as far as Chatham. I was called at eight o'clock in the morning to
take my watch the land being not far off, and we
heading for it. The wind changed to the Eastward
and it commenced to snow again. I awakened the
captain, telling him he had better come on deck.
Said he would, but as he did not thought best to get
the bearing and distance of Chatham Light. Soon after
it shut in. I went below, found the captain fast asleep,
awakened him by giving him quite a rough shake, and
told him he must come on deck. He came up; said
he, " Why didn't you call me before? " I replied,
that half an hour ago I did call him, and he should
have turned out. He said he knew nothing about it,
and was now at a loss to know where we were. I
told him how the Light bore and the distance I
judged it was away. He didn't appear more than
half awake, but thought we had better try to get back;

didn't like to try to cross the shoals. "No sir," I replied, "I will not consent to attempt returning; our sails are too poor for that, they will not stand the gale, and we shall unavoidably get on a lee shore, and stand a good chance to lose our lives. The only chance is to run before the wind, get over the shoals; we shall fetch up somewhere."

We put her before it, ran awhile, and I went along to see if any land was in sight; but instead of land, discovered breakers right ahead. The captain had the helm, and I went aft and told him quietly, so as not to alarm the passengers. I took the helm, while he went into the rigging to see what to make of them. It was still snowing thick. He had hardly got up thirty feet, before she struck the bottom hard. Another sea lifted her, and bang she went on the bottom. I sang out to him, "What shall we do?" Said he, "We must tack ship." I replied that she wouldn't stay, we must wear. I spoke to a man standing near the mast to drop the peak, and clapped the helm hard to port. The tide running strong to the eastward slued her around broadside to the wind and sea, which set her off to the windward, of the shoal, Then trimmed the sails aft, kept her to the windward half an hour, and tacked ship in hopes of weathering the shoal. Directly it was "breakers ahead!" and on both bows quite handy. Did not think it possible to get her about, she was so dull a sailor and it was so rough. .

The captain sent me aloft to look out the smoothest place, for he was going to put her on. Seeing but little difference, I told him to hard up; she struck heavy and went over. She now leaked badly, and we set both pumps going. Supposed it to be Pollock Rip, and gave her the course over the shoals. The wind moderating some and hauling to the southward, it soon stopped snowing and came in a thick fog. Passed Cape Pogue without knowing when. Kept sounding constantly, and soon began to shoalen the water very fast.

Sighted the shore and saw a very large rock. By this time tacked ship, stood off shore ; could not make out where we were nor did we know any such rock along the coast. Tacked and stood in for another look at it, but were no better satisfied than before. Stood off shore and ran awhile, then let the anchor go. It soon began to break away and clear up, and behold! here we were right off East Chop, and this terrible large rock was no larger than a hundred pound hay stack, but in the fog loomed up the size of a meetinghouse. The wind hauling to the wesward, got under way and ran into Edgartown. Lay here a few days, then started again arrived safely in New York.

Put the cargo out took another in for Bostou. Made one more voyage to Eastport, Me. Took a cargo for Richmond, Va., and a return freight for Boston, leaving there light from the scarcity of freight. Took a pilot

for Eastport; had favorable winds, and got down a
piece below. Mt. Desert; wind struck out northeast, a
strong breeze and thick weather. Our captain thought
best to try to make a harbor. Soon made the land
off the starboard bow, at a place called Long Island.
Sounded often and found deep water, running under
easy sail in the hope of finding a cove or bay in
which to anchor. It seemed to light up a little, and
a smoke ahead attracted our attention. We concluded
somebody inhabited there. It was not far off; kept
sounding, plenty of water, saw a little passage way
between two rocks ran in, found a nice little basin
and let go our anchor in the middle, our vessel just
swinging clear of the shore on all sides.

Seeing a small hut, landed and inquired where we
were. The old gent who occupied informed us the
place was called Burnt Coat, a place familiar to Down
Easters, When the wind came fair, put out and had a
good time down. A plenty of vessels were in waiting for plaster, taking it as fast as it came from up
river, and when a vessel hove in sight the boats
would board her and engage it. One day saw a
schooner coming down, and I was instructed to go to
her. Did so and engaged her cargo. She dropped her
anchor near us, but on the English side, while we
were lying on the American side.

It was near night and low water; the tide here ebbed
and flowed thirty feet. He gave his vessel a moderate

scope of cable. I told him to come alongside by daylight the next morning. We were around early, making preparations etc., but our expected plaster droger
was nowhere to be seen where the previous night she
had lain, nor anywhere among the fleet. It was calm
the fore part of the day; toward night saw a craft
coming in from the seaboard, which from her having
no topmasts, we correctly judged was the missing vessel. I boarded her as she came up, and learned that
during the night, as the tide came in her anchor was
tripped, and the wind blowing out to sea with the
current setting the same way, while they all slept
she quietly took her departure, without any legal
clearance and much against the wish of her crew.

We soon after took in the bulk of the plaster, a number of tons more than we should have done, which
brought the vessel very deep in the water, two planks
of the deck on each side being submerged even in
smooth water. Eight passengers, the families of two
Germans, came on board. Our water for vessel use
was in two large casks, lashed against the quarter-
deck bulkhead. I told the captain we should have a
barrel filled and placed below, in case of accident;
but he insisted that it was not necessary, and consequently went to sea without any additional. We came
along very well to the vicinity of Cape Cod. It was
our intention to land the passengers at the Vineyard,
that they might the more readily procure passage for

New York. Judging ourselves between Cape Cod and Nantucket, it came in thick with a strong breeze from the eastward. The Pilot objected to run; thought best to heave to for a while in hopes that 'twould clear up.

It was now about noon, and we lay to for an hour or more. The gale increased, and the mainsail was close-reefed after a severe struggle. The sea would fill up the bunt, and then we would empty out, and before hardly a point was knotted it would have to be repeated. Most of the afternoon was used up before it was properly secured. Got that and the bob jib on her, and shaped our course for the channel. Did the best we could to weather the shoal; the surf rolled over the decks, and it was not safe to leave the quarter deck at all. During the night one of the water-casks was stoven, and the water left in it was salted, and soon after the lashings of the other parted; the cask went to sea and we haven't seen it since. We thought we had passed the shoal, but on account of the breakers on every side, were unable to decide with any degree of certainty. We were glad to get her before the wind. Hauled down the reefed mainsail and furled it, also the bob jib was taken in, and we headed for Cape Henry.

We now felt the need of fresh water; thirteen of us all told, and several babies crying with thirst and none to help them. The wind was dead aft, and we scud under bare poles. We had but little to eat, had made a fire once only; boiled some meat, but it was so salt and our throats so husky, it was almost impossible to eat it. A sea struck the stern, stove the boat to pieces, started in all four dead-lights, and set her to leaking badly. By and by noticed that the vessel steered hard, requiring the whole lee or weather helm to make her mind it. Looked over the stern and found half the rudder was gone. The gale continued with unabated fury, and not a drop of rain had fallen. We knew we were getting handy to the capes of Virginia, and if the wind did not fall off we should soon be on the beach.

The captain was below. I went down to get something from an under berth, and heard the water rushing down in a torrent. Soon discovered that the seam was open on deck, under the edge of the bulk-head, and that the quarter deck was working considerably. With a case knife lashed to a pole tried the opening, and found it was quite bad. Happening to have a quantity of oakum on board, with the point of the knife-blade ran it the length of the seam a number of courses, which the descending current sucked in; afterwards pressed it in solid, stopping most of the water out. It had to be done from the quarter deck.

We were fearful that we should have to scud her on shore. I went below and told the captain that we must be well, in as the water had a slight colored ap-

pearance; that he had better come up and see what
was to be done. I told him that in my judgment we
had better heave to; it was too risky running longer.
This he said he dared not to undertake, for fear the
heel of the mast would jump out, rip up the deck, and
we all go to the bottom. It was now the fourth day
since putting away, and the wind had not varied a
single point of the compass. In the afternoon it began
to thunder and lighten. Lit up some, the wind and
sea going down a trifle. The land was but a short
distance to leeward, eight or ten miles to the northward of Cape Henry. It now moderated, and we hove
the vessel to under a reefed forestaysail. Lay a
while, when the wind hauled to the northward, and
we put away for Cape Henry. We soon saw a pilot
boat running in from sea-board; he came up and asked
if we wanted a pilot. We replied that we did, but
that water was wanted more, for we had been out
four days. He replied that he had ten gallons only,
for it was some days since he had been up, but we
should have part of it. Our boat was gone, and his
little skiff would not live a moment in so rough a sea,
What was to be done? As often quoted, "Necessity is
the mother of invention." They took a fender from
the pilot boat, attached a rope and threw it overboard.
We got our vessel dead to leeward, it drifted to us,
took the end of the line in, then a keg was bent on
and we hauled it on board. It came in a good time,
for we were thirsty enough.

Not able to weather the cape, came to anchor under its lee, in company with the pilot boat. The next day got under way and attempted to beat up. Seeing a topsail schooner from Norfolk, bound to Baltimore, we forelaid to speak him and set a signal for him to heave to. He did so. We asked for water, telling him we were in a suffering condition for the want of it, and asked if he had any to spare. He replied that he had, and ordered our boat to come after it. We told him we had no boat, that he must launch his yawl and bring it to us. Said he, " I cannot stop to bother, with a fair wind;" squared his yards and put her off for Baltimore.

Not long after saw a little negro droger coming down James River. We spoke him and asked if he had plenty of fresh water, for we were short; had been for some days. He replied, " Yaw, massa; me got half barrel." We then asked if he would sell or give us some; if so to launch his log canoe and bring us a part of it. He brought us all he had, with his face shining, and grinning with laughter at the prospect of doing a kind act. He said, " Here, massa, be all the water we hab; take him, massa." " No, no," I replied, " we will not take it all; you will need it." " No, massa, you take de water; we's be up to Norfolk fore night, but you no be dar, — take de whole." We forced him to keep a bucket full, and some bread and meat were added; our grateful thoughts followed the generous souled colored man, as he left us in the enjoyment of his gift. Now, let me ask, which of the two men showed the most of a civilized nature? The old darkey had a black face, but his heart was, we thought, far whiter than the pale face brute who didn't like to bother.

The next day reached Norfolk. Purchased a new boat, and employed the services of a calker and carpenter who repaired damages. When the calker began his job, he asked what fool had been at work on the seam. Hearing this, a little sprung, I hastily replied, "You poor devil, had you been on board when that job was done you would have thought your last day had come; on my knees, from the quarter deck that seam was calked, three feet under water." His views were suddenly changed; said that being the case, it was well done. From there we went to Richmond, discharged our cargo which weighed one hundred and nineteen tons, while the vessel only measured seventy-five, and returned light to New York, when a freight was loaded for Boston.

This was the last trip I made in that craft. From her I joined a neat and pretty schooner, called the Gen. Greene, under my old captain, who would always have me if good wages could secure me; for he appeared to think full as well of me in these days as when we were peddling fish and clams in Connecticut, during my early apprenticeship. We advertised for freight and

passengers for New York. In a few days were loaded
and made a safe passage. Took freight back again,
and afterwards made several trips to Philadelphia,
Charlestown and Savannah, continuing in a general
coastwise business about three years.

On one of these trips we left New York, bound to
Philadelphia, with a fresh breeze from the north west.
Ran along to the southward with the land in sight,
came down within twenty or thirty miles of Cape Ann
and hove her to, heading off shore, thinking we might
be handy to the Cape by daylight. At twelve o'clock
at night went on deck to take my watch. Had only
been on a short time, when a pilot boat was observed
working towards us. This I reported to the captain,
and asked if I should take a pilot. He replied that it
would be best. The boat soon came up, and the pilot
hailed to know where we were bound and if a pilot
was wanted. Told him yes; he came on board, gave
the course for Cape May and ordered sail made upon
the vessel, I asked him if he knew where we were,
and he replied that he knew pretty near, but had not
seen the land for a number of days. I told him that
at dark we judged ourselves such a distance (naming
the number of miles), from the cape, and thought it
most proper not to increase the sail for fear of getting
to far to leeward, without being able to see the land.
He said that he knew his business.

From running under a foresail only, hoisted the

mainsail and set the jib. She was going a good lick. The captain remained below until his watch expired. I told the pilot that it was my humble opinion he was making trouble for all hands; but he was not to be convinced till daylight dawned, when from aloft I saw we had left Cape May many miles to the windward of us, and informed him of the interesting fact. We had to double reef fore and aft, hauled sharp on the wind, and beat the livelong day. Just at night got so that, with a favoring breeze, we were enabled to run up. This bit of experience only served to strengthen my convictions, that some pilots didn't know any more than they should.

While in this craft had frequent opportunities of visiting home. The suits referred to were progressing slowly, being carried from one court to another, but I managed to keep clear up to the present time; believing that in general a great deal more of law is practiced than justice, which was perfectly demonstrated before these pending cases were settled, previous to which settlement I was pressed as a witness in a trial instituted against Mr. Coffin by the captain of our old ship. I was put upon the stand. Upon being questioned, told the counsel it was but little I knew of the affair, and very much disliked to tell that. . Being asked if I thought Mr. Coffin went ashore of his own accord, replied that I thought he did not; that he was ordered to take his things and leave, under pen-

alty of being forced to by a file of soldiers, while Mr.
C. protested his helplessness, in a foreign country
without money. The attorney than asked if Mr. Coffin
was really desirous of continuing the voyage. I replied that was my opinion. Was then asked if Mr.
C. was a good officer, who, knowing his duty, performed it, etc., to all of which I was obliged to answer
in the affirmative, as also many other questions which
were replied to with regard to truth, but in as few
words calculated to injure the feelings of any as I
could place them.

There were men who, in giving their evidence, did
so with a view to promotion ; this I did not care for,
as I had no axe to grind, no hobby horse to ride.
My whaling was done ; but not so with some others,
and it was somewhat amusing to hear the individuals,
who had been almost starved at times on the voyage,
express so fully the great respect they entertained for
their old captain, on account of his uniform kindness
and the generous quantity and quality of provisions he
had always furnished. The consequence was, our
evidence didn't exactly correspond. During the cross-
questioning I was asked if what I said in regard to
Mr. C.'s unwillingness to be discharged was correct,
and if I had heard him express himself willing to perform the voyage. In reply, I claimed to be correct, but
had not heard him say it in so many words. Now the
spectators thought I had a foul anchor, sure. Was

asked, if I never heard him say so, how did I know
what his wishes were? " Sir, we often hear quoted
"Silence gives consent;" if, then, he was not willing
to go the voyage, why did he object to leaving?" At
this reply a laugh ran around the court room, and I
was excused from testifying further.

The case was soon after thrown out of court, and
though much money had been expended, none but the
lawyers received the benefit of it.

As the period was near at hand, anticipated in my
boyish fancies, in being the possessor of a snug and
comfortable house of my own, I determined to make a
purchase, having previously secured a lot pleasantly
situated in the immediate vicinity of the village. The
building which I thought would suit our wishes was
but partially completed, and it having been attached
for debts and offered for sale I applied to the agent,
and was told that it could be bought for two hundred
dollars. I considered it too much, as the building
would have to be removed, and to complete it would
require additional expense. I offered one hundred and
forty, which was refused. I had let forty dollars to a
friend of mine ; called upon him, informed him of my
intention to buy, and that the money would be needed
in case I did. Finally engaged him to go to the
parties who had attached the property, and make the
purchase of them ; which he very kindly did, buying
it for only one hundred dollars, the residue of which I
paid him.

Shortly after, meeting the agent, he informed me that I had lost a chance of buying a good building cheap. Told me it had been bought, and such a time was allowed for removing it. I told him it was all right, that my lot was all ready for it to be placed upon it. " What ! " said he, " was it bought for you ?" I replied that it was. " Well, you have got it pretty slick after all."

A few days after, it was placed on the lot. I then shipped on board the sloop Five Sisters, Thomas Milton commander, to enter the lumber business. Our vessel lay on the south side of Town Wharf ; a ship was at the end, heading to the southwest. The wind was from the southward and westward, and we were getting under way to leave port. The captain ordered the mainsail, which was quite new to be hoisted. We up with it, headed northwest. I asked if he intended getting under way as she lay. He said yes " Well," said I, " if you do you will cut a caper. " Why ? " said he. I replied that we should be afoul of the ship and tear our sail ; that we had better run out the kedge and pull by, as the tide was setting down. He said no, and ordered the jib hoisted and our bows shoved off with a pole. The current swept us across the ship's bows, and the jibboom and all the rigging went through the mainsail, splitting it into quarters. We ran out an anchor (which appeared very much like locking the cellar door after the meat barrels had been emptied), and after some heaving. cleared from the snarl, up jib, and headed out of the harbor.

Had a strong, fair wind, and soon went to work repairing the torn sail. We happened to have plenty of needles and twine, but only one palm. By the time we got down to Chatham it was ready to hoist, and favorable winds soon carried us down to Gooseborough, Me. Ran up to the mouth of a river and let the anchor go. The captain was going on shore; said he shouldn't trouble the vessel much, as he had trading to do, and that when the cargo was taken in to put on all the help needed; to live well, — if it was not on the vessel, to buy it. He was to inform me when the lumber was procured for the cargo.

It was my intention to buy what was required to complete my house, which, at the going rate, would be taken by freight with our load. I went to the mill to make a raft; formed the acquaintance of the proprietor, and finding he was a great lover of sea yarns, often endeavored to entertain him. Two men assisted me in rafting the lumber. One day the lumber broker said to me. "Come here; I want you to give me some of your good stories." I told him it was too busy times; I must get the raft completed. Said he, "Never mind your working, I will turn on a man to do the work." So seated myself and commenced to do his bidding, and kept it up till the raft was finished.

Took the raft down river and loaded it, and in a

day or two went after another. I bought some for
my own use and made a small raft of it. "Now,"
said he, "while my men work for you I want some
more stories." I told him that I had bought a house,
that the lumber marked for myself was to put into it;
"But said I, "I see you have any quantity of refuse
lumber piled around. I want you to give some of it
to me, for the coarse finishing up about the premises."
He replied that I could have as much as I desired,
and ordered one of his men to get it out for sending
down with my raft. I was telling him big stories all
the while, when, looking up perceived a large pile
had collected under the industry of his man, and told
him to hold on. Said he, "You have not enough yet;
you are welcome to all you will take" The pile was
increased, when I told him again to stop, for my con-
science would not allow me to take all there was in
the yard. After getting home, found that I had enough
and some left, beside a pig-sty and other outbuildings.

The mainsail was repaired in good shape and rebent,
when we made a start for Gooseborough again, under
charge of Mr. A. a gentleman who was to accompany
us for the purpose of purchasing lumber for a salt works.
We had the wind southwest. Had passed Chatham. I
had the helm, trying to keep along as straight as possible, but it was a hard craft to steer. Half a mile
ahead of us was a fishing pinkey at anchor, and the
captain proposed running as near as he could, in order

to get a fish. I told him he had better take the helm himself, but said he, "Do as I bid you and it will be all right." The captain stood forward with a junk of salt pork in his hand ready to throw to the· fisherman. As he got handy, hailed the only man on deck, the others being at dinner, to throw a codfish on board. Getting too near, the captain ,sung out, "Hard to port." The fish struck on deck, and about the same time our vessel struck the pinkey aft, taking off all her quarter-boards, unhung the main boom, and completely stripped her as we passed along. By this the crew were out of the forecastle, and not a little cursing and swearing was indulged in till we were out of the reach of their voices. As we never met afterwards, the bill of damages has not been presented; but I thought it a foolish experiment and should not have been attempted, for we had no business so near her. But accidents will happen in the best regulated families.

It was so rugged the quality. of the fish was not tested on that day. We had for a passenger old Parson Thaxter, whom we were to land at Boston on his way to Hingham. Just previous to our arrival, the boy who did the cooking on board was getting breakfast early in the morning. The parson was out, combing his white locks preparatory to landing, and by some means threw a loose one into the frying-pan, where the boy had his pork in ,slices frying. It was not observed by him, and the fish was accordingly cooked and breakfast announced. Mr. Arey and the captain were seated on one side of the table, and myself opposite. I noticed something in the platter did not exactly " look like lard, or even fish," but said nothing. The captain assisted Mr. A. to a good piece and asked me if I would have some, I replied that as my appetite was poor, I should have to decline. He helped himself and then gave another piece to Mr. A. they thought it very nice. Presently, in attempting to get a little more, the captain hauled out the lock of the old parson's hair, he having a short time before left the vessel. He looked at it and asked what it was. I replied that it had the appearance of hair. " Well," said he, " it is not to be wondered that your appetite failed, if you had seen it," and they both began to feel rather qualmish in the region of their bread-baskets. Said he, " Why didn't you tell us ? " I replied that I didn't wish for them to loose a good breakfast, or have the boy punished ; so in the hope that it would pass off unnoticed, kept still.

We continued our voyage down East, loaded quickly, and returned homeward. Had thick southerly weather for a number of days ; sometimes laying our course, at others making much lee way, and somtimes running to leward of her course. The vessel loaded by the head the cabin filled with laths and shingles. We did not see the sun for the passage. One day while at

dinner, Mr. Arey asked the captain where he calculated to fall in. He told him the Highlands of Cape
Cod would be sight at three o'clock. I couldn't help
laughing, our calculations differed so widely.

Mr. Arey asked why I laughed, and my reasons
were given. Began to sound about one o'clock, still
thick ; kept sounding, but got no bottom with the scope
of line we used. Kept running with a good lookout.
It was now three o'clock, no land in sight, and not
any soundings. Capt. Milton said he had been
mistaken, and asked what my reckonings were. I told
him at six o'clock we should be up to Cape Ann. At
five o'clock thought I would go aloft and take a survey, having often observed that objects may be dis-
cerned over the top of fog-banks. Had but reached
the cross-trees and looked away to the northward, when
I saw the land under our lee beam. At first said
nothing, to assure myself what it was, and tracking the
land made it to be Cape Ann. I then informed them
that Cape Ann was off our lee beam. The captain
said it must be the highlands of Cape Cod. "Then,"
said I, "it has undergone a strange revolution, for
instead of running north and south it runs east and
west." The fog soon lifting, it was soon settled that
my calculations were correct.

A fleet of lumbermen and wood-carriers soon appeared,
as the fog drifted off to leward. They were light and
bounded to Maine from Boston, which fully decided

that we were still in the vicinity of Cape Ann, or these vessels would not have been in their present position. The next day reached the Cape, and the day following arrived at home.

Made one more trip in this vessel; during my absence had carpenters at work completing my house. We returned safely from the last cruise, though we had a rough time. We lost both anchors, and met with some trifling incidents, but nothing worthy of note. But before I leave this stage of my narrative, let me remark that our captain was a noble-hearted man, generous to a fault, and the best man to victual a crew I ever sailed with. He was one of those very sanguine men who,

> " If convinced against his will
> Would be of the same opinion still."

CHAPTER XX.

THE workmen employed upon my house had progressed so well that we were enabled to move in
the first of November, where, in the society of my
family I remained till late in the spring. The first
fruit of our union was a boy, with whom we were considerably elated.

During the previous Winter, a brig was cast ashore to
the southward of Gay Head light. The cargo was
taken out, and the vessel stripped of her spars and rigging to her lower mast, and abandoned. A severe gale
occuring soon after, she was driven up high and dry at
low water and sold at auction, Thomas Mayhew of
Edgartown, and Capt. Seth Daggett of Holmes' Hole
being the purchasers. These gentlemen agreed with
ten or twelve persons from the former village to get
her off. I was one of the number. Everything requi-
site was conveyed by water, and on the shore we constructed a rude cloth shanty; in dry weather it answered very well, but in rainy times, it was rather
leaky.

Among our party we had a lad about fourteen years
of age, who served us as steward, and a real smart

198

little fellow he was, full of life and fun, always ready
to answer to the call when Theodore was wanted He
was a son of Robert Winpenny ; in disposition cheerful
and somewhat given to singing ; though usually harp-
ing on the same tune and words, which made so deep
an impression on my own mind they still are fresh in
memory. For the edification of any of you who are
fond of choice selections, I will repeat this little bal-
lad ;

> " Down by the Taunton river,
> Where the herrings sport and play,
> You be home you Yankee lubber,
> You be home by Christmas day."

Our young steward had some distance to go after
water, procuring it from a spring in the edge of a
swamp. One day he went out ; had nearly gained the
spring when he was brought to a halt by a very singular noise. Listening very attentively for a moment,
he proceeded with cautious footsteps in the direction
from which the sound came. On approaching quite
near the spring, saw a hideous-looking black snake in
the act of bringing its charms to bear upon a helpless
robin immediately in front of him. The reptile was
whipping his tail through the air, producing a noise
very much resembling a spinning-wheel ; (young folks
can ask their mothers what that instrument is.)

The eye of the snake was fastened upon his intended
prey, and the bird trembling and fluttering seemed perfectly under the control of his magnetic power. I

think the charmer must have been a full-blooded medium. But Theodore dispatched the snake and delivered the bird from his dangerous enemy. The boy was taught a lesson which, through years of eventful life gave him a very decided aversion to snakes in the grass, either of the brute or human species. Snakes were abundant in this region of country, frequently paying us visits, which was very annoying, particularly after we had retired.

The wreck was found bedded in the sand, nearly up to her chain-bolts. Screws were placed under, first digging for solid foundations on which to rest them. After awhile raised and blocked her up. She was very heavy-timbered, and two hundred tons burthen. Finally were ready to lay the ways, but awaiting a favorable time to launch on account of the rugged shore, just such a day being absolutely necessary. The next night it came on to blow, and the morning revealed to us the interesting fact that our work must be done over again, as the blocking had been undermined, and the vessel in the condition in which we found her weeks before.

After many days of hard dragging, supposed her all regular again. The gale arose and the swell swept up the shore in its vengeance, and down she went the second time. As before, she was again raised, and now we really thought she soon would be floating. In place of the short timber used amidship heretofore, we now introduced her rudder which was very large and strong, and we felt quite secure. But this, too, was destined to be a failure ; a strong westerly gale destroyed all our carefully arranged plans, and the third time our work was vain and fruitless. We pretty much concluded that she would lay her bones there forever, but Mr. Mayhew thought different. As he had already expended much money he was determined to get her off, if it took all the vessel was worth to accomplish it. A hard rain set in about this time and our shanty leaked like a scive. All hands concluded we would endeavor to procure lodgings in the barn owned by Mr. Skiff, the light-keeper at that time. Unfortunately for us, one of our number was a colored man, but a good old soul as ever lived. Upon application for the barn for lodgings, Mr. Skiff flatly refused, because he was with us; squealing out, " If that darned nigger should sleep on that 'ere hay, my old hoss would snuff and snort and wouldn't touch a mouthful of it." So we returned to our old quarters, consoling ourselves with the reflection that we didn't love him any better than he did negroes.

Our rudder, that we had so much depended upon as a support for the vessel was reported the next morning, a part lying on the rocks at Squibnocket light, and the balance on the north side of Gay Head, at a place called Cooper's Landing. With a boat one was brought back, and the other was brought overland by

an ox-team. This done, a part of the company went to
work to raise the vessel again, and two or three sent
to town with the boat after provisions

As the season advanced, the weather became more
settled, work progressed finely and at last we were ready
to lay the ways. The rudder was spliced and hung,
some little arrangements were made in the way of sails
when we should require them, and then a successful
launch was made. Keeping account of all the distance
she had at different times been raised it amounted in
the aggregate to twenty-one feet. The Summer was
now drawing to a close, our job was nearly completed
and no accident had occured to any of us. But not
so with those who were at work in the clay pits near
by, and a little to the northward. Thinking that perhaps my services may some day be required, the incident may as well be cited.

Quite a number of the natives were grubbing out the
clay for shipment, when one in the act of striking a
heavy blow with the instrument used for that purpose,
accidentally fetched it down upon the shoulder of a
squaw, making her yell with pain. She soon made
rapid strides for the house. While others were in search
of a horse to send to Edgartown for the well-known
bone-setter, Jeremiah Pease, Esq., I went to the house.
I asked if the shoulder was broken ; she thought it
was, as the fingers were stiff, and her arm could not be
lifted. I asked if I could examine her arm. " O yes,

dear a suz." I gently crowded the part most injured, and in went the fractured bone with a snap. " Now," said I " raise your arm." She did so without trouble and I was pronounced a skillful surgeon. This was my first experience, but I did not tell them so. Have had no practice since.

The vessel was now at the end of the ways but still not floating. We had carried out anchors to haul out by, and had made some arrangements for putting on sail when necessary. Hove the anchor up and made sail, and in two days reached the harbor, the vessel leaking freely. She was fitted up slightly for the purpose of being taken to Portland in hopes of selling her to her former owners. Discharged all the men with the exception of three beside myself, who, with the owners were to proceed in the vessel. We reached Cape Cod, took a head wind and ran into Province-town, where, being taken sick and each day growing worse, I took passage in a western-bound lobster vessel toward home. Was landed on Cape Pogue, and brought to town by the kindness of the light-keeper. Did not feel very well for some time, but finally recovered and was just as good at new. It being now well towards Fall, remained about home till Spring opened.

CHAPTER XXI.

ARLY in· March took the fishing smack Fair Lady for a season's work off the south side of Nan.tucket Island. A neighbor of mine who was familiar with the cruising ground accompanied me. Our craft was a clever little vessel, only eleven tons burthen, cedar bottom, built slinker fashion, or, better understood, lap-streak. She was decked over ten feet forward, which served as a cabin, having two berths below, with a small fireplace for cooking the grub. Was not very high in the posts, for if we occupied a seat six inches high, our heads would come in contact with the deck above.

On our first cruise out, was rather fearful of her abilities, not being full-decked, and it being an un-usually rough place, but soon found she was to be trusted. She was a very able boat on top of the seas, seldom shipping more than a bucketful of water, how-ever rough it was. Cod and halibut were very plenty and we considered ourselves No. 1 fishermen, usually filling our well in a single day. The fish were carried to New Bedford, always finding a ready market.

204

Would procure bait at home and go out again. We wound up the business the last of June, having made more money for the length of time than ever before or since.

Worked at home when anything offered until May of the following year. Was not much driven with business, and consequently took life quite easy for a while.

Capt. Lot Norton, about this time, was bound to the coast of Labrador fishing; I shipped with him, made the voyage and returned, being gone about four months, that length of time being the shortest to entitle those who fitted her to the U. S. bounty. We all hove together and made a good season's work. Capt. Norton was a pious old man, and many a good meeting we had on board the Bethel fisherman, frequently receiving visitors from other vessels to our Sunday services. Our fish were disposed of to vessels bound up the Mediterranean, and we returned in ballast. I told Capt. N. if nothing prevented I would go with him next season.

Some time in the latter part of the next March, Capt. E. Ripley had charge of a coaster; was coming from New York. It was a dark, thick, foggy night, and by some mistake in his reckonings he ran his craft on a ledge of rocks to the northward of Gay Head, called "The Devil's Bridge." She struck several times but beat over and sank in five fathoms of water. The crew took to the boat and landed at Tarpaulin Cove. With others whom he employed, I went to the scene of the disaster, and, if you . like, I will give you a little account of our expedition.

THE WRECK.

CHAPTER XXII.

THE cargo of the wreck was composed of baled cotton, copper sheets, (for ship bottoms) in boxes, a quantity of corn in bulk, and cotton cloth. We first secured two vessels, in which the necessary equipments for raising were taken, with the party who were to assist. Two long spars and chain cables and a dozen men accompanied these vessels.

Found upon our arrival only the mastheads above water. Placed one chain under forward, the other under aft, with a vessel on each side of the sunken one. Lashed the spars across the decks of the three, took a turn of the chain around the spars, put a large oak heaver on to turn the spars, making what sailors call a Spanish windlass. Hove a heavy strain at dead low water. The tide began to rise, and we hoped that by full sea she would be lifted clear of the rocks; if so, we intended to get her in a little nearer shore and repeat the experiment.

As the tide came in, she did not appear to come up at all. Found that one of our vessels was too small to take her part of the strain, and was gradually being

207

brought under as fast as the tide arose. We held on until her deck was under, and were obliged to slack up and take the small one out. We went to Nantucket, hired a larger craft, and rigged as before. It was now quite rugged, and the current was quite strong, so waited until it became smoother and hove down again. Before high water gave us a chance to test our new arrangement it came on to blow hard from the westward, parted the cables, and very gladly we left her to lie a while longer. Dispatched a vessel to New Bedford, procured a ship's cable, and in a suitable time rigged again, not willing to give up beat. Hove down once more, getting every inch that was possible at low water. At about full sea she began to move. Sail was made on the vessels, with a fair tide headed to the northward: took her clear of the rocks and headed down Vineyard Sound. After a few hours reached Lambert's Cove, and the tide coming in ahead anchored.

The wind coming up strong from the westward, hove in a terrible sea. We chafed and ground so badly, had to slack up and let her sink to the bottom. Shortly after, hove her up again, bringing her tafrail and knightheads above water, and started with her for Edgartown. Arrived all right and unloaded the damaged cargo. The owners made us an offer for saving the property, but not being satisfactory, we sent a responsible man to Boston, who libelled the vessel and cargo.

It went into Court in due time, and after a while a settlement was made, the lawyers as usual, taking the lion's share. The expenses of litigation being adjusted we made one dollar and twelve cents per day.

From the action of the copper upon the corn, it was supposed that it might be poisoned. One of our citizens, somewhat interested in the purchase of the corn, wishing to test it in this respect, did so in rather a queer way. He had in his family a Kanaka, who accompanied him to this country on his last voyage at sea. He concluded that he would have a quantity of the corn boiled and fed out to the native on trial, saying that if it did not produce his death it would be safe to feed his hogs upon it. It was tried, and no visible injury resulting, the corn fetched at auction twelve cents per bushel.

The town presented the appearance of one grand general washing day, most every fence about being used for the purpose of spreading cotton cloth to dry. Thus ended my first experience in the wrecking business. Quite soon after, however, had a plenty of it to do.

CHAPTER XXIII.

T had now got to be so late in the season, gave up my previous intention of another Labrador voyage. Early one morning it was noised around town that a large topsail schooner was high and dry on the south end of the Island. Soon learned that she was from the West Indies, loaded with rum and molasses,— a very inviting cargo to those fond of the " critter." She was not bilged ; the cargo was all removed, and with a strong wind on shore she was cast above low water mark. Mr. Thomas Mayhew contracted with her owners to get her off for a certain amount. He hired eight or ten with myself to assist on the job. In a small craft he owned we took all the apparatus required and began work on her. The beach being high, did not raise her much Laid our ways to launch, but made a failure the first time. As the weather was rather catchy, it getting along towards Fall, it took a number of days waiting for a good chance to operate. At last launched her into the surf, but she did not float. Had an anchor out some distance from the shore. Now it began to blow and snow. Sail was made on her. Had just hoisted the mainsail when the sheet parted, the boom struck the shroud, broke it in two pieces, also tore the sail. Took in the broken boom and sail on deck. As the combers rolled in, her bows would jump, but still she hung by the stern. As the tide arose we hove at the windlass, and just at night she started. Dropped the sails, hove up the anchor, ran from the shore a short distance, and let three anchors go. We were not anxious to drag out to sea, as we had neither water nor provisions in the vessel.

The wind canted to the northward and a very cold night set in. As the chimney had previously been caved in, we could have no fire, and take it altogether it looked rather dismal for comfort. By and by, the wind changing to the westward, got underway and reached the harbor of E. the next day.

Very soon after, there was a smack called the Lookout, cast ashore in very nearly the same spot as the one just launched. No one was on board and her crew were supposed to be lost. T. Mayhew bought her, and I went with him to assist in getting her off, and also brought her to town. Mr. Mayhew used to take many such jobs; he was a remarkable man for ingenious inventions in this line, and always extremely unwilling to abandon a job once undertaken. Would hang until his efforts were crowned with success. I frequently afterwards accompanied him during his excursions, dragging for lost anchors, which at that period was quite a lucrative occupation. On one occasion with two vessels, one called the Surprise, under my charge, and the Lookout, on board of which was Mr. Mayhew, were on the south side of the Vineyard, where we had been sweeping for cables. Suddenly it shut in a dense fog, both vessels being at that time under sail. Soon it was impossible to discern the other craft. My partner said, " What are we now to do ? " I replied that I should take the vessel into the harbor. " Well," said he, " you will have to do it for all my help, for I don't know the first thing in such a fog." I told him to hunt up a line suitable for sounding. He found only a small scup line with its sinker, weighing less than a quarter of a pound. Among so many shoals and reefs, with the current setting from two and half to three knots, it was but a poor substitute for a deep sea lead.

We kept along to the north-east, hauled up to the northward, and with the intention of giving Cape Pogue a wide berth, ran for some time, till satisfied I could fetch by. Let her come in stays, heading for, as I calculated, the Gurnet, or Eel Pond opening. My partner asked " Where are you now ? " I replied that if he would heave the lead as I luffed up, I would tell him. Soon judged where we were, and as we shoaled the water upon the opposite shore, told him to keep a sharp lookout. As yet nothing but fog could be seen.

He asked me again where we would fetch up. I then said to him, "Soon we will drop the anchor, and to-morrow morning when the fog has cleared we shall be lying between the shores of Chappaquiddic and Collector Norton's house, and Mayhew's vessel will be to the northward of us, on her beam ends on the flats at low water. Sure enough next morning, when I went on deck, I saw it just as I had imagined. Called up my "pard," and said "What do you see?" With great surprise he said, "It is just as you predicted; you would out-devil the old fellow himself for a pilot in a foggy time." I thought it would not have so happened again in a thousand years.

CHAPTER XXIV.

UNCLE JETHRO MAKES A HARBOR AT PORT SANDERS AND
FORMS THE ACQUAINTANCE OF A WANDERING TRIBE.

O N the first of May started on a voyage to Labrador with my old friend Capt. Lot Norton. We
made a harbor at a place called Port Sanders,
Newfoundland. There had been a snow-storm, and it
still lay upon the ground two feet deep. It was now
raining some, but cleared off in the afternoon, and from
the woods a little inland, saw a smoke arising. Knowing this part of the country to be uninhabited for many
miles around, our curiosity was a little aroused to find
the meaning of it. Our boat was launched and paddled
toward the shore. When we landed, and as we
approached the fire, saw a large Dutch blanket hanging
from the trees, and upon near approach found it used
as a protection from wind and rain, for the comfort
of fourteen men, women and children who were stretched
on the ground under its lee. The snow had been
scraped away and bows from the trees were spread
for a bed, on which, feet to the fire, this singular
looking group were very contentedly enjoying themselves. Upon accosting them, found that they could

214

speak our language. We asked an old white-headed veteran if there was not danger of taking cold. He replied, "If our feet are kept warm there is no danger to be apprehended." They were the members of a single family who were moving, as frequently they did, from one harbor to another, picking up what game came in their way, and living from year to year in the same manner, not owning any house and having no regular abiding place.

Among them I noticed a little fellow, peeping over his protector's shoulder to get a look at us as we talked, and asking her who appeared to be his mamma if I couldn't have him to take home with me, he burst into tears and opened his mouth so that I surely thought the whole of the upper part of his head was coming off, — and ours too, as he loudly yelled. We asked how they got along with the very aged ones, who did not appear able to do much travelling, and were told that they were carried by the younger ones on their backs. The only articles of property we could see consisted of the blanket, two old guns, a copper kettle and a small quarter of what appeared to be beef. It was what they called caribou of the deer family.

We asked the old gent if he would sell us a part of it, and he said we were welcome to the whole of it. We told him that would not do; they must keep some of it for supper and breakfast. He replied,

"never mind us ; we have good guns and know how
to use them." A part was taken and found to be
very nice. The old man was asked to accompany us
on board, and we would pay for it. He was helped
to the boat, and a little something was given him to
drink, which pleased him. Also gave him bread, molasses, and a bucket of Indian meal ; he had never seen
any meal before, and was told how to prepare it for
eating. As he was about to leave gave him another
drink. "Now," said he, "I suppose my squaw would
like a small drink ; " so we filled a bottle and told him
to give a little all round. We did not land again,
but three years after we put into the westward, three
hundred miles distant, at a place called Cod Bay ; a
boat came to us, in which were two squaws, one of
whom, addressing myself, asked for meal. I asked her
what she knew about meal, she replied, "You once
gave me some ; I remember you very well, sir." They
had baskets for sale, of their own make, which she
insisted upon my buying. She said, "Have you children ? " I informed her I had three when I left home.
"Well," said she, "you must have three baskets, and
in return I will take meal." We had plenty and the
trade was made. She eyed me closely, and, observing
it, I asked her where she ever saw me before. She
told me she was one of the party at Port Sanders, &c.

Our voyage was continued, and we reached the usual
fishing grounds. I had heard some of our crew speak

of a certain individual as being there in command of
a vessel, with whom I once sailed. One day, in
approaching our vessel as I was coming in from boat
fishing, saw him on the deck of our craft, and informed
the man with me of it. He said he was so far off,
could not tell him ; I replied that I should know his
ashes after he was burned. All hands were in the
cabin. Our boat was secured, and my partner had
followed the others down. The visitor had shaken
hands with those whom he knew, when my partner
told him there was another coming who knew him.
He looked at me as I started into the cabin, and asked
me if I knew him. Said I, " Yes, sir ; to my sorrow."
He asked where I had ever seen him, and I told of a
certain voyage we made together. Our captain agreed
to let him have our fish, his business being to purchase,
and to Brader Basin we went to deliver them. We
had a remarkably handsome lot, as we thought, but as
we passed them on board the other vessel, the captain,
standing at the scales, discarded many as poor. I
was on his deck helping to pile up the scales, and
handled them rather faster than suited him, and he
asked to have me removed and another sent to take
my place. Our captain asked his reasons for the
exchange. I came back to my own vessel, but did
not like the idea of his sending back so many fish. Directl-
ly a very large one that ; on account of a hole cu tin its
nape, he refused to take, was returned and, with the

other refused was kentched below by itself. · Along towards noon a boat landed alongside our craft, and two ladies got out who were going to pay a visit to the captain of the brig alongside of us. Consequently he ·was obliged to leave the work of weighing, to entertain them in his cabin, but asked another captain who was on board to attend to the scales in his absence. Told him to take no fish but what were good. Seeing so fine an opportunity, I told the boys to keep a good look out and let me know if the captain of the brig came on deck. · I jumped into the hold, and while others passed up the fish as they had been doing, I went to the pile of castaways and passed them out at fast as I could. Worked some time, when the repors was made of the uprising of the man I did not just then care to see, for on the top of the scales was that identical large fish, fair in sight! He came directly to the scales, took the fish up and hailed me, saying, "Did I not send this fish back once?" I answered that he did. "Well," said he, "you have been sending up the refuse fish, have you not?" Told him I had, and if he had not come just as he did they would have been all stowed in his hold, as it was a few only were left. He looked at me pretty hard, when I returned the look and told him that I rather thought now he knew me. He then told the captain of our vessel that if "that Ripley" was allowed in the hold again, he would take no more fish. The rest of the cargo was delivered, and drafts were signed by him upon his owners. We started for home, arrived sometime in September, remained about one month, and then took a trip to a warmer clime.

CHAPTER XXV.

THE first of October, shipped on board sloop Hero, and went to Boston to take in an assorted cargo for Charleston, S. C. Usually when goods came aboard, the question was asked, if we were going direct to sea or intended making a stop at Edgartown or elsewhere We always told them, if we had freight to be delivered, should stop. A boy used sometimes to come with goods for shipment; the captain would sign the bills of lading, and no questions were asked in relation to our stopping.

We completed taking in cargo and started for E. The most valuable portion of the cargo was insured, without any specifications in regard to stoppages on our passage. We came up to Cape Pogue and fell in with Sch. Eliza Jane, Capt. V. Pease commanding, bound to Philadelphia with a number of passengers on board. He was a *driver* and sailed his vessel on shares, and, as the saying is, allowed no grass to grow on his vessel's bottom by lying around. We had just tide enough to weather Cape Pogue and get into the

220

harbor of E. Ran in, and in less than two hours had landed what freight we had to deliver, and were ready for a start. The wind holding ahead, thought it advisable not to attempt to get out; were delayed a number of days, waiting for a suitable time. One afternoon the wind died out, and Capt. P. got under way and worked up to Tarpauline Cove. We still remained Next morning took a light breeze and started. The wind was south-east; and occasionaly it would blow a little harder, then calm down again. So we worked along the best we could. We got nearly abreast the cove, when the breeze struck across the sound, and the fleet lying there took their anchors, set sail and came out. Soon discovered the Eliza Jane in the crowd; was within a mile of her, and went out on the same tide with her, the captain recognizing us as as well we did him. Before dark passed Nomans Land, and before twelve o'clock were put to skudding under the head of a square sail, and wind enough at that. The gale lasted all the next day, and hauled from the north-east a little to the southward, still blowing a living gale and finally changing to the south-east. Were compelled to heave to under a storm trysail, on the port tack, headed to the westward. Kept her so for five days and nights, a heavy sea on, and we loaded very deep. The wind started a few points more to the southward. My watch below until twelve o'clock was then called. As the captain was about to repair to

the cabin, I asked him if it would not be well to
wear ship; told him if I had charge should certainly
do so, for we had been on the same tack five days
and nights, and might have overrun our calculations.
He insisted there was no necessity for it, as neither
sand, rocks nor shoals endangered us, and went below.
In my watch was a Swede, as good a fellow when
awake as ever was, but one of these drowsy individuals who could not stay anywhere without dropping
asleep. I stood abaft the binnacle, watching by compass
the course the vessel was making. At first the sea
was tumbling in amidships over the main deck; had
been watching but a few moments when I observed
that the sea rolled along more quartering. Again
scanned the compass to see if her course had been
altered, but found her still heading as last seen. The
conclusion I hastily formed was that we had gone into
shoal water. I took the lead, gave it a cast, and found
less than three fathom. Clapping the helm in the
weather bucket, grabbed the Swede and sent him
forward fast enough to be certain he was awake,
ordered the trysail halliards let go, and called all hands.
Up came the captain, who wanted to know what the
matter was. I told him there was matter enough;
"we are going on shore, sir!" Said he! "How much
water have you?" I replied, "Three fathom, sir;
some help here as quick as possible; let's get the
trysail to leeward of the halliards." We got the clew

around, got the sheet partly aft, hoisted it up and trimmed flat. "Now, sir," said I, "we will try the lead." Did so, and found a quarter less there. He was perfectly astonished. Now the old swell gave it to us right in the face and eyes; it was neck or nothing, but we deepened the waters lowly. Put a reefed jib on her and gained a little, carrying it until ten the next morning, when it blew so heavy that we had to furl it, keeping her dead to leeward the while. Sounded and found fifteen fathoms. Let her lie, catching it just as she could. We suppose the shoal to be Barnegat. The wind going down and hauling to the westward, made sail and shaped our course for Cape Hatteras. Got pretty well up with the cape, and another easterly gale came on. She was put under close sail again, three reefs in the main sail and reefed jib. Finding we could not weather Hatteras, wore ship stood northward, and in the forenoon thought best to go into Hampton Roads. We bore away for Cape Henry and ran in by, the wind slanting to the southward a point or two. The captain had the helm. Ran in by the right and went into Lynn Haven Bay, just to the south of Cape Henry. I said that I hoped he was not going to anchor up there. He said he was: he did not like to run a dozen miles out of his way when he was ready to start again. I told him we had plenty of time, and a safe anchorage was of a great deal more consequence than a few miles. He said when the wind

came fair we should have less distance to run. I told
him no time would be lost by keeping up; if he
anchored here he would find his mistake before morning dawned. We came to anchor there it was now
quite late in the afternoon; the captain went below and
turned in. Our sails were reefed sea-fashion, not very
snug. I told the men we would shake out the reefs
and· put them in better shape, and everything was put
in good order for what soldiers would call, a stampede;
for I felt it in my bones such would be the case before
long. I told the Swede to take the first watch, thinking he would be most likely to keep awake the
earlier part of the night. Told him to keep watch
of the weather and the other man who was to relieve
him was told the same. Intending to stand the last
watch myself I went below and turned in all standing,
except my boots and hat. Had been below about an
hour when the Swede came down and hurridly in;
formed me that a gale was blowing on shore.

When I first awoke, thought perhaps he had been
asleep, and the wind had changed without his knowledge. She was heading nearly west, and it was
blowing violently with her lee rail most under water
She had not yet swung to her anchor, so I knew
the wind had just come round, as the Swede said.
It was instantaneous. She headed it soon; all hands
were called. As the breakers were right under our
lee, hove ahead on the cable. Hove short, up with

the reefed mainsail, and took the anchor. She was pitching her bows under; fell off to the westward. We up jib and put her to it, heading to the north-west on the starboard tack. It was so rough, she made but little headway. I seated myself to the leeward of the rudder head, and perceived that she was gaining toward the shore. I told the captain she would hardly fetch by the point. He said it was impossible to tack, and two wear ship were just as bad; the only thing to be done was to trust luck and keep her running, thinking possibly she might go clear. We had got to the very turn, and if there had been half a cable's length to spare it would have been all right; but as she settled into the hollow of a sea, she struck hard, another sea lifted her, and down she would go again. Let the sails run and dropped the anchor, in the hope that she was over the worse bar and would hold on. A decent scope of cable was payed out, by which she was held; still, every time she went down, bang! she would strike. The captain stood holding on by the main rigging. I asked him if he intended to let her knock her bottom out there, to which he replied that he didn't know what was to be done. I told him I did. "Then," replied he, "do it as quick as you can." I ordered the boys forward to slip the cable, set the jib, and and haul the sheet flat aft amidships. She slued around and headed for the shore; a heavy sea struck her stern, forging her ahead some distance, and another kept her her going inshore. The jib would not allow her to broach to, and headlong she fetched up, hard and fast on the beach.

The first heavy sea after grounding stove in one of the deadlights near my berth. I grabbed my well-stuffed canvass mattress, on deck with it, doubled it up, secured a rope to it, then ordered one of the hands to pass it over the stern; from the dead light window I caught it, then it was tompled over and I hauled it up to the window, and fitting tightly, as long as it lasted it kept the water from dashing in. It was for awhile the tightest deadlight we had. The other beds were also prepared in the same manner, in case of further emergency. The first gave out before long and was replaced by another, and as often as they failed us another was used, until there was none left. Then used for the same purpose an old sky sail. We had not bilged, and we thought we were doing very well, but just then a tremendous sea came and the three other dead lights all went in at once. Had only time to get our chest and dunnage on deck, before the cabin filled with water. They were placed forward of the windlass. The sea was breaking from stem to stern. It was now midnight. When we ran on the tide was up; it had now begun to ebb, and we were some little distance from the shore, the shoal water extending out pretty well. In the morning judged it to be low water, and preparations for landing were being made. Our small boat would not live a moment in so heavy a sea, but we soon began to cut and contrive. We had a large spar on deck we sometimes used for a fender alongside. To this we bent on a rope and threw it overboard, the sea washing it up until it grounded before on shore. With the end of the rope in my hand, went out on the end of the, bowsprit, and carefully making it fast a little slack, I dropped down to the water, and as a good sized sea swept along allowed myself to be carried with it, the rope rendering through my hands. The rest of the crew landed in the same manner.

It was now somewhat cold, being the sixteenth of October. Anxious to find some place of refuge, went in search of a house. A large pond lay between us and the upland, and following around to westward, we struck a road which conducted us up to a dwelling. We went in and found it occupied by an old bachelor who was a planter, and owned quite a drove of animals which at that time were called "slaves." We were welcomed. A large fire was going up the old fashioned chimney, composed of logs six feet long and large in proportion, but we did not complain. The old gent wanted to know where we came from and all the particulars of our shipwreck, but was told after we had procured something to eat and a little sleep, would tell him all about it. He said we must make ourselves as comfortable as possible, and soon breakfast would be ready. As we became thawed out, with one accord a drowsiness crept over us, and before a greatwhile we all slumbered and slept. He aroused us, and we sat down to a nice warm breakfast of hoe-cakes, fried bacon and coffee, prepared by the negro servants. We enjoyed our meal hugely, and afterwards, by permission of our host, went to bed. While regaling ourselves with the sleep so much needed, the negroes dried our clothing in good shape.

The gale continued, with unabated fury for a number of days, but as it moderated we began to think about changing our boarding place. Soon after, with the help of the slaves, unbent the sails, took them on shore, and constructed a tent. Saved the cargo and stored it in the tent. We tore down a small wooden fish-house near the shore, and with the boards closed up the dead lights, and went to work pumping out the water, which was soon accomplished. As it was now thought best to carry an anchor out, and our boat was not near large enough, we went six miles up to the eastward, to a river where was kept a large seining boat. We started with her toward the vessel, but before getting back the wind prevented us from carrying out our intention. Were compelled to land and haul the boat up for safety. Returned on foot to the wreck, and found it nearly floating, but as the waves hove in each one drove her further up, until at last she was nearly to the highest part of the beach. Was rolling heavily, first one way then the other, with the force of the sea and wind. We were afraid she might be left heeling to seaboard ; so we boarded her, took the kedge anchor over the high beach, and with the end of the halser attached to the main halliards, hove her down, deck in shore, and secured her. When the tide went out she was all right. Northerly winds and sea banked the sand around her fearfully. The cargo in a damaged condition was advertised and sold at auction, at a considerable loss to the shippers.

The weather after some time being more favorable, our captain contracted with the planter to get the vessel off; but he would only make the attempt in case he could secure my assistance, as he knew but little about launching vessels. The captain told me what he had agreed on, and finally with the assistance of the slaves, we went to work. Trees were cut down, and hewn off on two sides flat. We had heavers instead of screws, but after some hard work raised her sufficiently to place the ways underneath. I objected to the timber used for the purpose, properly judging it not strong enough to bear the heft of the vessel, but the " boss " thought he knew about this better than I did, so, let him try it. Greased the ways and started her down, but slucing a little on her way to the water, brought an unequal bearing and down went the timber, and the vessel in the sand and water, by far in a worse condition than when we started her; for now all the work done must be done in the wet. Other and larger trees were cut, squared and placed under, and in due time she was launched down, only hanging by the stern on shore while her bows floated. We all hands turned on at high water to heave her clear of the land, but for some time worked in vain; she would not go. Gave it up for a higher tide. Shortly a good breeze blowing off shore, boarded and set her sails; everything drew, but yet she started not, and as the tide began to fall, we left her. Soon, however, a terrible rumbling voice was heard among the pine trees; it was a squall of wind, and when it struck the vessel with her sails still hoisted, it made her groan—but it took her off and she swung at her anchor.

We boarded her, lowered their sails, and made pre-paration to go up to Norfolk. A person had been on board whom we had secured as a pilot, but afterwards found he was a very ignorant one, to say the least. The captain gave the charge up to him and went be-low. We started. Could hardly lay our course; the pilot had the helm; the tide was ahead; I saw we were sagging down toward a Lightboat, and spoke to the pilot about it. He said there was no Lightboat there, that it was only a vessel at anchor I knew better, for I had seen her ever since we had been on shore. I then told him he was no pilot, and didn't know but little anyway. We tacked ship and stood

to the southward. I kept heaving the lead, and as we
shoaled the water, would come in stays. We had
made a few tacks and were standing to the westward.
The pale beams of the moon threw their light over
the water, and looking toward the land I saw Hampton Bar, which fact I communicated to the pilot and
told him we had better go about. He said we were
not near it yet, but I insisted that I was correct, and
that if we did not soon tack we should be on the bottom. I had the helm now myself. He took the lead
and line, hove one cast, while I watched the line as
it ran out and preceived it to be shoal water. Clapped the helm hard down; she shot ahead a considerable,
which brought her upon the bar. The captain came
on deck and wanted to know if we were cast away
again. I told him we had a jackass for a pilot, for
he liked to have run the lightboat down, and didn't
know there was such a thing about here, and now has
run us on the bar. The sails were instantly lowered
and an anchor carried out from the port bow; but not
being able to heave her off by that, took the anchor
and carried it out astern. Soon brought her to it and
went up to Norfolk, arriving there Dec. 23d We
were unable to get any person, white or black, bond
or free, to go to work on our repairs, as every individual must have three days for the Christmas holidays.
From what I saw of it, concluded one day was to get
ready for it, one was for a good drunk, and the third

to become sober. The calkers and carpenters then
turned out and put the vessel in good order.

The captain one day was on shore. I was aloft fitting some part of the rigging, expecting soon to start
for Richmond. A gentlemen came on board and inquired for the captain, and being told that he was on
shore, then asked to see the mate. I immediately
came down and shook hands with him, calling him by
his name. He returned the greeting in a cordial manner, but with some surprise said, "You have the
advantage of me, sir; you appear to know me, but I
do not recollect that I have ever met you before."
"Nor have you, sir, and I have no advantage of you
in the least; I have not seen you before, nor did I
know there was such a man in existence, but allow
me to ask if you did not once have a brother by the
name of Butler, who resided on Marthas Vineyard?"
He said that Matthew Butler was his brother, and did
once live there "Well," said I, you resemble him
so closely, if I had not known him to be among the dead,
should have supposed you were the man; but as you
are not, you must be his brother. This gentleman being a pilot by profession, his services were engaged
to take us up. We loaded with flour for Charleston,
arrived with it, and, before the river closed up, made
a start for Santee for a cargo of rough rice, which
was taken in bulk. Continued in the rice business
during the Winter, sometimes loading at Santee, some
times at Tranquility and Wamboo.

Some of the rivers visited we were obliged to cut our way up, the foliage was so dense along their margins; but the season was good and the business very agreeable.

In the Spring took in a cargo of staves on freight, for an ·individual of our acquaintance who had been trading, and in part payment took staves for the New York market. We come out of Georgetown with a heavy wind, stood off shore fifteen or eighteen hours, a heavy swell heaving in toward the land. The captain said we had better let her come around and stand in. I told him we could not yet fetch by Cape Hatteras, but not agreeing with me, did as he was disposed and tacked. I asked him how far off he judged us to be. He named the distance, and I told him he was twelve or fifteen miles further out than my calculations brought me. I gave as my reason that the old swell had impeded our headway at least one knot an hour, but he doubted it. The wind soon came out fair. We were under whole sail, it was somewhat smoky and thick, and I felt anything but comfortable for fear of what I thought was ahead. I maintained a good look-out, and not long after I discovered right on our track a shoal. Reported this to the captain, who had the helm at the time, and asked him if he was aware that he was running on to Lookout Shoal. He replied that he was not, nor was I. I then told him that the shoal was right ahead, and that if we did not alter the

course we should surely strike it. Said he, "I never
in all my life saw such a man as you are; you are
always borrowing trouble for yourself and everybody
else." I told him how much better it was to avoid
trouble before getting into it. He told me to take the
helm. and he would hunt up all the line there. was on
board the vessel and see if he could find any bottom.
He was some time in the cabin. . At last, getting out
of patience, I told him that a short line was all that
he would need, and that would be useless if he did
not come soon.. He came up and bent the line on,
sounded, and found but a few fathoms.

It had now begun to thunder and lighten, and away
to the northward and westward saw an ugly squall
coming down for us. Let every sail run flat to the
deck. It came on violently, but in a few moments it
had passed and left us perfectly becalmed. Hoisted
the jib and main-sail, a heavy swell meanwhile rolling us toward the shoal now quite handy to us. We
took a large sweep or oar over the quarter, and on
the bow opposite, and after a while swept her bows
to the swell. Cleared away the cables and anchors,
ready to let go if necessary. Took the sweeps, on
each side doubled manned, and began to pull for dear
life; were just able to hold our own. She was pitching, first her bows under, then the stern boat was terribly thumped. It was now a little past noon. We
kept on pulling, feeling rather ugly and, if I correctly

remember, somewhat inclined to be impudent. Just at sunset a little breeze came to our assistance, and gladly our sweeps were replaced in their lashings and we shot out clear of the corner of the dreaded shoal. Looking to see the trim of the sheets aft, observed the clue of the mainsail was about gone, foom the slatting it had taken. Lowered it down, put in a single reef, and re-set it. Finally passed Cape Hatteras, arriving in a few days at New York. The staves were sold, fetching twenty-five cts. less than was required to pay freighting.

Returned to the Vineyard some time in July. The underwriters had refused to pay the insurance on our outward bound voyage. Claiming that our vessel had deviated on the passage, the agent, Mr. John Thaxter, went to Boston, returning soon after for my deposition, which was subsequently taken into court, and I was in hopes to be able to avoid having any-thing further to do in the affair. Some few months after, however, I was summoned to come into Court, to be holden in Boston. I went, was put upon the stand, and questioned very closely in regard to the voyage. When asked if I was mate and where I kept the log, replied that I was, for want of a better man, and that my log was in my head. In the course of my evidence, I gave the details of the passage and pro-ceedings to the best of my knowledge and recollection, much as it has already been given to you. In refer-ence to my being able to idetify the Eliza Jane, already alluded to, I was questioned and cross-questioned by the several attorneys for nearly three hours. Said one, "We presume if she had left the cove the previous day, any other craft would have answered your purpose equally as well." Much was said relative to the distance the vessels were apart. I had observed one. of the lawyers frequently consult a paper on the desk before him, and concluded it must be the deposition formerly given. I asked him if it was not. He replied that it was, and that I must follow a bee-line or I should be trapped. In reply I told him that he rather had the advantage of me, but when it was given months before, I gave it with a view to the truth as it existed; but thinking the affair would be adjusted without any further proceedings on my part, I might have allowed some of the circumstances to pass from memory, and might vary a trifle in some subjects, but added, that however true this might be, the vessel I could never be mistaken in, from her peculiar construction. She was built at first for a sloop, was bought on the stocks previous to her being planked, — she was sawed apart amidships, and a piece put in the middle made her very crooked or moon-shaped, — when her masts were put in they pitched aft, the main truck being over the topsail. I knew her well, and if any one was not satisfied with my ability, I would take them to Goldsborough and show them the stumps from which her timbers and planking were cut. It was de-

cided by the jury that I knew the vessel, and a verdict
was rendered in favor of the owners of our vessel, on
the ground that it being unsafe for a superior vessel
to our own to make a passage under the same circumstances as ourselves, was not sufficient reason to rob
shippers of their just demands for insurance on the
losses which could not be foreseen or prevented; the
result being mainly attributed to the weight of the evidence I was able to impart. In the way of compen-
sation for my valuable services, the owners did not
give me as much as a plug of tobaco, though perfectly
familar with my propensity and strong attachment to,
the weed, and which no doubt so disgusted me, that
in less than twenty years time I abondoned the habit
of its use entirely. Have since enjoyed a good degree
of health, besides conferring a great favor on my ever
devoted companion, the bosom friend of my earlier
life.

The next season took charge of this vessel, and if
you care to hear it, will tell you where I went.

CHAPTER XXVI.

STARTED for Boston May 1st., with eight men and a boy, to fit for a fishing voyage, and in a few days put to sea. Our first land fall was Gaba-russe, Cape Breton, where we dropped anchor on account of bad weather and head winds. A boat containing a man shoved off to us; he had with him a bag of young pigs which were offered for sale. As we did not care for them, declined to purchase, but after considerable talk he was offered and gladly accepted, half a bushel of meal for two of them, and told us to take more of them if we desired. I told him two were as many as I knew what to do with. He put them on board, the boy placed them in a barrel and was ordered to take care of them. Sometimes we would give them fresh fish; they enjoyed stripping it up and throve nicely. We had a good run, made a stop at Bay of Islands, procured wood, water, boat spars, etc., and continued the passage, arriving at Brador Gulch, where our fishing was to be prosecuted. We were quite successful during the season. The latter

238

part of June had a visit from a gentleman residing by a neighboring harbor. He said he had noticed we had pigs running around on the rocks on shore, and was very desirous of buying them. He said he wanted them dreadfully. We refused to let them go; for on the fourth of July we intended to celebrate, and the pigs were to be butchered for the dinner. On the first day of the month, myself with a number of the men having some business to transact with the gentleman alluded to, we went to his house. Found .him with his wife at home. I happened to be seated near the outer door, alone, while the others were together on the opposite side of the room. The lady came along and took a seat by me and commenced to speak of matters and things in general, but I perceived she had something on her mind of more than ordinary interest. Directly, in a quiet and subdued voice, bending her form most gracefully to me, she attempted to give utterance to the burden of her heart. Just think of the painful suspense in that moment of seeming inability to control her emotions, or express her longing desires ! Taking a long breath the tremulous lips began to move, and, with her bright eyes resting on mine, hardly less brilliant (just about that time), she broke forth, "Mister, ain't you the man that owns the pigs ? " I told her that I was. " Well," said she, " I do want them dreadfully ; I will pay you any price for them." I told her that I could not think of disposing of them, that we had anticipated having a general good time on

the fourth of July, and must have the pigs for our dinner. "Oh!" said she, "it is too cruel to kill those
little hogs, and I do want them so badly." I saw
that I should be unable to prevail against such plead-
ings, and finally, with considerable reluctance, gave
way with a promise that she might have one if she
was so much in want of one. But still I found her
only partially satisfied; once more she turned to me
and very natnrally asked if they were not of different
sexes. I replied that they were. "Is it not then best
to let me have them both and not destroy the family
relation?" At last, finding her not to be put off, I
agreed, if she would pay the boy two dollars for his
care of them, she might have them, as I did not wish
to speculate in pigs, and was not anxious to make
anything out of them. Her countenance was radiant.
and she gave me such a smile of gratitude that I was
glad I let her have them; although no doubt if she
had not been an exceedingly handsome lady, we should
have eaten them as we had hoped to. For this act of
kindness I was severly censured when I returned to
the vessel and informed the crew of what I had done,
one going so far as threaten to inform the owners that
I had sold the vessel's provision for speculative purposes. I told him the trouble would be saved him.
When we arrived at home I told the circumstances to
Mr. Timothy Coffin, our owner, and he said he wished
I had taken *all* the pigs down and given them away.

In the Fall saw the pigs; they had grown nicely, and I tried to buy them of the lady again. She said I hadn't money enough on board the vessel to tempt her to part with them. These were the first pigs ever introduced there, and I afterwards learned that they became quite plentiful.

Our fish were now sold, with the exception of about eighty quintals, still awaiting a fair day to complete the drying. A spell of wet easterly weather hung on, and finally concluded the vessel in waiting had better proceed on her voyage, and we would take the fish on board our vessel and start for home. We did so with a fair wind the following morning. In the afternoon it commenced to blow. At four o'clock I took the helm, and, the gale increasing, the vessel was brought to scudding under a square sail. Eleven hours it had been blowing and the sea was extremely dangerous. When my trick at the wheel was up, could find none who dared relieve me. They claimed, that, as I was more accustomed to the vessel, it was unsafe to trust her with any one else, for fear that she might broach to, when it would be all up with us. Nineteen hours I remained without a spell, occasionally taking a mouthful of grub or a hasty drink as I could catch it. After it moderated gave up the helm. Were now off Cod Roy harbor, which we entered and for a number of blowy days lay at our anchors. I told our folks it would be best to secure the ballast by flooring over with boards, to prevent it from shifting in case of more rugged weather which we might reasonably look for before getting home. They all preferred to go out gunning, and did so. During their absence, I went into the hold, laid a floor, and with the spurs stanchioned down solid, made it quite secure. But for fear the stanchions between the deck and flooring might work loose with the motion of the vessel, I cut hinges from the legs of old boots, and nailed them to the heads of the posts and to the deck as a preventive. The wind came fair and we made sail, shaping our course for Scatterce, a ninety miles run.

With a fair wind and plenty of it, we were going off a pretty good jog. It began to blow still harder, and thicken up, and there was every appearance of a South-easter. Not long were we in forming the conclusion that sail must be reduced and the vessel hove to. Now we wished we had more sea-room. We wore ship, and headed off on the starboard tack; in place of the mainsail set the trysail, with the jib reefed. Soon had to take in the jib, and it had become dangerous to longer remain on deck. Lashed the helm to the lee and all hands went below and closed the gangway slide. It was a hard old night; a sea would strike and heave her lee rail all under. Some of us looked rather pale in the vicinity of the gills, somewhat fearful of the ballast shifting. It was a queer looking group, seated on the cabin floor during that tempestuous

night. I told them there was much more danger to be
apprehended from what lay to leeward of us, than from
the ballast in our hold. We only had forty miles drift-
way before we should be piled up on the shore, where
the coast was rock-bound, in some places more than
five hundred feet high. The next forenoon the wind
suddenly changed to the opposite direction, blowing a
gale from that quarter, but st ll we did not dare to
run. Laid to twelve hours for the sea to get regulated,
then put her before it, under the sail we had hove to
under.

Had a good passage the rest of the way home,
arriving the first of September. I remained about home
for some time, occupying myself in various ways,
sometimes by short trips on the water, or lumping
along shore. I took two more voyages to the Straits,
which I shall slightly allude to. My usual occupation,
on land for more than thirty years, was the fitting of
rigging on board wrecked vessels, and for the fleet of
whalers then owned by our citizens.

There were three of us who were in the gang, a Mr.
Godfrey, acting as our boss until his death when I
took the position, though Mr. G. had never been in
the habit of cutting a gang of rigging without consult-
ing me. Mr. Collins was our third man until quite a
number of years since, previous, however, to the decease
of our boss, when a Mr. Courtney, a retired whaleman
lent us his assistance. Mr. C. was one of the best

whalemen that ever went in the head of a boat, and
had the satisfaction of seeing thick blood flow a great
many times under the accuracy of his aim, and even
now it is somewhat amusing to listen to his ' bloody
stories of ugly whales, and how they were at last
forced· to surrender. It rarely happens that he spends
an evening in a crowd, but that several voyages are
made and enough oil taken to supply a pretty quick
market. Not only did I find employment as rigger,
but ·in a general way performed a little of all sorts
relating to fitting awayships or stripping them on their
return, or sometimes acting as oil watcher at night.
also assisted in breaking out the cargo, etc., etc. ; any
thing which offered which was remunerative and re-
spectable.

Many accidents have attended me during my exper-
ence, since I left a regular sea-faring life. More than
once have I missed my footing, and come from aloof
much quicker than I went ·up ; yet through the kind
ness of a watchful ˙ Providence, have escaped without
any permanent injury to limb, or disfiguring of features.
Am still able to walk erect and enjoy the gratifying
reflection that I am not really bad-looking for a man
of eighty. Not a great many years ago, while engaged in fitting the rigging on board a vessel, a rope
above me parted, letting a large sized hoisting block
plump upon my head ; two hours after, the same
thing was repeated, and yet I sustained my senses

though for a while in both instances I saw stars distinctly. Not a few times have I barely escaped with my life from similar accidents, besides the capsizing of boats, and a general variety of mishaps incidental to an individuals destined to be always in harm's way. About three years ago a little incident happened so out of the regular course of things, and the means of restoring myself being strictly original and withal not extremely expensive, I think it best for the benefit of my hearers and of mankind generally, to speak of it. I was at work by the day on a ship fitting for a whaling voyage. As was our usual custom, at noon all hands knocked off, and went for our dinners. For the want of anything better, my good woman had fried some bacon. Somewhat hungry, (for hard work will most always make person so), seated myself, and doubtless displayed some eagerness in putting my allowance away. Not having a great many teeth with which to chew my food, and, as I have since discovered, but a very diminutive swallow. In the act of taking a piece of meat it became fixed in the throat so tightly that it was very much feared I should strangle myself. A person was dispatched with all haste for Prof. Mayberry, one of our eminent M. D.'s of our village. He arrived and considering it quite essential to provide himself with some surgical instruments, in order to relieve me from my critical condition, returned to his office, less than half a mile distant.

In the mean time I became somewhat impatient, for although the doctor was not gone long, it seemed to me an age, and at last I became so exasperated that I took a long slender stick, split the end, picked up a dirty piece of rag that happened to be lying round loose, drew apart into the stick, winding a quantity over the end, and then leading the outer end to the end of the stick that was to be held in my hand. I gave it a desperate shove. The meat went down and I got up; did not stop to finish the dinner, but took my hat and started for the ship. Met the doctor on his way, when I told him it was so near one o'clock (the turning on time where I worked), that I couldn't stop any longer for him. Went to work as usual. Since that time, when strangling, I always use the same means and do not send for the doctor.

CHAPTER XXVII.

YOU will pardon me, my friends, for passing over two voyages to Labrador, which should have been noticed earlier in this narrative, having been accomplished forty years ago, more or less. One of these voyages was in a miserable old hulk without sails and rigging, just fit for old junk. As usual went to Boston for our supplies, etc., with a crew of nine men. Had a common passage, nothing remarkable occurring as far as Canso, near Halifax. The wind then came ahead and rain set in ; the main sail became very heavy and sagged so that the bolt rope parted, and down it came, leaving a foot or two of the sail aloft with the gaff. Sent them down, and mended the sail the best we could before running it up again. The rain changed to a thick fog, and we thought best to endeavor to find a harbor.

We knew hardly anything in regard to the lay of the land, knew not any place convenient for our purpose, but kept along maintaining a good look out. Soon land hove in sight close aboard of us, right ahead.

Tacked ship, stood to the wind south, and directly land was ahead and under our lee. It appeared that by some means we had entered a river. Made short tacks, until a ledge of rocks directly ahead and in the middle of the passage caused us to let go the anchor. The shore was not in sight now, so dense was the fog. It was high water. We went below and made a good fire to dry and warm ourselves. Not a great while after, a boat came alongside, in which was a gentleman who asked where we were from. We told him we were from Boston ; had been in about one hour. He thought we must have had an excellent pilot ; could not conceive how we had been able to enter the river at all, so thickly were rocks and shoals scattered about. He remarked that he had lived in this vicinity thirty years, and never before had he seen a vessel in there. He was more than surprised when, in reply to a question, we told him we had not grounded nor struck a rock. I thought then if we had been in some nice vessel we should not have fared so well ; but the old hulk was not worth pounding against rocks. This man was a pilot along the coast, but he acknowledged that with his experience and knowledge of the river he could not have succeeded as well as we in our ignorance had done. I thought the poet was perfectly correct when he wrote,

" When ignorance is bliss, 'tis folly to be wise."

We waited three days for an opportunity to be taken

out. The pilot started with us on about three-quarter tide, as in case we lodged on the rocks, full tide would lift us clear. The name of the harbor, was Peter the Great, lying N. N. E. from Canso Light, thirty or forty miles distant. We continued on our voyage, which was successfully accomplished without anything transpiring worthy of note, except our safe arrival at home where we remained through the Winter, starting the following Spring on another trip in the good old brig Planter.

Our brig was under the command of Thomas Fisher, with a crew of twelve men and a boy. Had a favorable run to the gut of Canso, which divides Cape Breton from Nova Scotia. We made the ice, and for security went into the harbor of Jesterco. In a few days had company by the arrival of another fishing vessel. From the extremely friendly relations existing between her commander and our own, we judged them members of the same masonic fraternity, which subsequently proved correct.

The ice was from three to four feet thick, and from Newfoundland across to where we lay, one field of ice stretched out before the eye. We had waited some time for it to clear out. One afternoon the captain of the other vessel came on board. Our skipper said to Capt. Cassno, "How long do you think it will be before this ice melts or goes out so that we can proceed on our voyage?" He replied that if we waited

for it to melt or break up, we should get no opportunity for fishing during the season. That, to me, was
anything but an agreeable feature, but soon he somewhat alleged my apprehensions by stating, that in less
than twenty-four hours the ice would all disappear by
sinking. "You will observe, by holding a piece up to
the light, that it is very porous and has a dark colored
appearance, a sure indication that it will not long
remain." The wind was to the southward ; consequently
if the ice moved, it would have to drift directly to
windward, from the lay of the land, the outlet being
only ten miles wide to the northward.

At daylight in the morning went aloft, looked over
the beach, and no ice could be discovered. Both vessels got under way and sailed, with a strong fair wind
going at the rate of seven or eight miles an hour,
Saw no ice during our further passage ; now where
did it go ? I say it sank, and persons who contend
that the theory of fields of ice sinking is false, will
please tell us, if it does not sink what does become
of it ?

On the passage I noticed the skipper and Uncle
Oliver were fitting a large lot of gear. I looked on a
few minutes, and observed to the shipper that I presumed he and Mr. Norton intended to catch all the
fish during the cruise. Said he, "O, no ! but let me
tell you we do expect to catch one-half that comes on
board the vessel." I replied that they would not if I

had my health. Said he, "I wonder if you don't expect to be 'high hook?'" I replied, "That is just what I do expect; if I can not will not go home in the vessel. Sooner will I work my passage on some other one." Said he, "Then I rather guess we shall make a saving of grub, for if you keep your word we shall have one less to provision ; for I never was beat in my life." I told him he had never had me to fish against. "No," said he. "but I've had a blamed sight smarter man to try it on." He had the advantage of me by his buying the stern of the boat privelige, while I had to fish in the bows, but at the close of the season I led him in count ten hundred and forty-two fish. "Now," said I "Captain Fisher, I think you will have to vitual me a little longer ; I shall take the passage with you." It did not set well on his stomach. Uncle Oliver was behind me over two thousand, I having taken during the six weeks of fishing thirteen thousand fish to my line, which, with those of the rest of the crew, were salted and brought to Boston green, and were cured at Galloupe's Island, down the harbor. When we had completed the task, with the exception of about eighty quintal, — as a party had chartered the brig for a West India voyage, the owners were exceeding anxious to get the balance dried and brought up to market. The captain was an owner also. He ordered all who could work to advantage to turn on to washing out. While thus engaged

I noticed that the heat from the sun was very oppres-
sive ; it was terribly hot. I remarked to the skipper
that unless the fish already spread were taken care of,
the heat would destroy them. As he paid no heed to
my expression of opinion, I repeated the suggestion
and told him they would surely become sunburnt. He
only told me that I appeared to have a great deal to
say about the fish. I told him that as I owned the
largest portion of them, my self-interest made me
speak. He said, "Let them burn and be hanged, for
every fish must be washed to-day." The washing was
continued to the end of the chapter. Towards night
went on shore to fagot, or pile the fish. As we took
them by the tail it dropped off in our hands, and as
we attempted to gather them by placing the hand under
them, the napes would fall to the ground. They didn't
amount to much. Often did I afterward fill a bushel
basket with the burnt fish, and exchange them with
the farmers for a small pail of milk. What were not
thus disposed of we left upon the Island, not considering them worth gathering up. I told the skipper that
he ought to be compelled to pay for them; I think so
still. His reply was that he was not aware how hot
the sun was. The balance of the cargo was taken to
the city and sold, and after a six months absence we
returned to our homes.

CHAPTER XXVIII.

ND now, having wearied my listeners with the recital of some of the most important scenes in my checkered life, there is but little more to add. The sun of my declining years is sinking fast. The trembling limb and wrinkled brow tell me in words that is difficult to misinterpret, that the glass of my mortal voyage has about run out. Three score and ten has been numbered, and the eighteenth of July, 1873, will be eighty years since my birth. It is not strange that I sometimes feel to appropriate the words of the poet:

> "My days are gliding swiftly by,
> And I a pilgrim stranger."

By and by it will be said of me, as of most of my childhood's companions, "he is gone;" but if prepared to meet the great change that awaits the family of Earth, it is not particularly material at just what moment we are summoned. Hoping to be reunited in a brighter world than this, I draw the narrative to a close.

THE WOODBINE SERIES.

By Mrs. Madaline Leslie. 4 vols. Each, $1.25.

This set of books, by this well-known author, is in her best style, and well adapted to the young.

1.
Live and Learn.

An authentic narrative. An old sailor gives the story of his life, the key-note of which is "Perseverance." It teaches the young how to learn by experience.

2.
The Governor's Pardon.

The facts in this book were related to the author in visits to the "Massachusetts State Prison," "Blackwell's Island," &c. It tells a tale of great vicissitudes, — life at its beginnings degraded; then enobled by Christian faith; shipwrecked afterwards, but through mercy brought back to noble influences.

3.
Paul Barton : THE DRUNKARD'S SON AND DAUGHTER.

A Temperance Story. The agony, suffering, and degradation inflicted by drunkenness are forcibly set forth, and the power of religion in sustaining those who are made the victims of the drunkard's passions.

4.
Walter and Frank; OR, THE APTHORP FARM.

Walter and Frank are brought together to instruct each other in what contentment and happiness consist. The former, though poor, has good health, and a heart touched with the love of Jesus; the latter lives in a palace, tired of his surroundings, because he has up to the first interview with Walter remained ignorant of the nature of religion. Their friendship issues in a happy consummation.

THE RAINFORD SERIES.

By GLANCE GAYLORD.   4 vols.   16mo.   Each, $1.50.

The above set of books, by the late Warren Ives Bradley, under the cognomen of "Glance Gaylord," author of "Culm Rock," "After Years,' "Dora Dean," "Boys at Dr. Murray's," &c., is one of the best set of books ever published. They are eminently fitted for Sabbath School libraries.

1.
Gilbert Starr and his Lessons.

It is full of life and animation; tells of boating and other sports of schoolboy life. The trials of a boy, who is led into captivity by his pride and ambition, and, at last, by the influence of a schoolmate, struggles out into freedom.

2.
Gilbert's Last Summer at Rainford.

This continues the story of "Gilbert Starr," "Ray Hunter," and "Perry Kent," through another term at school, and everywhere is as full of interest as the first. They are not overdrawn, but characters such as we meet with every day.

3.
Will Rood's Friendship.

Will is a country boy who goes to the city, and enters the family of a school friend, being employed by this friend's father. A very severe trial comes to him, which he meets with rare heroism. The whole is decidedly good, and sure to interest any boy.

4.
Jack Arcombe.

Jack is a poor boy adopted by a wealthy gentleman as a companion for an invalid son, with whom he is educated, and remains until the bankruptcy of his patron, and afterwards cares for his friend. The whole is a story of deep interest.

CORWIN'S NEST SERIES;

OR, STORIES OF BESSIE AND JANIE. 6 vols. 18mo.   Each, 75 cents

This charming set of books really consists of two series, one for girls and one for boys; but all of them recommend sound morality and earnest piety.

Corwin's Nest Series. FOR GIRLS. 3 vols. 18mo. $2.25.

    LITTLE TOT'S LESSON.   BIRTH-DAY PARTY.
        BESSIE AND THE SQUIRRELS.

Corwin's Nest Series. FOR BOYS. 3 vols., in box. $2.25.

    CHILDREN AT PLAY.   WHISTLING HORACE.
        JAMIE AND HIS PONY.

Corwin's Nest Series. FOR GIRLS AND BOYS. 6 vols. 18mo. $4.50.

    LITTLE TOT'S LESSON.   CHILDREN AT PLAY.
    BIRTH-DAY PARTY.   WHISTLING HORACE.
    BESSIE AND THE SQUIRRELS.   JAMIE AND HIS PONY.

They are put up in boxes of three or six, as may best please the purchaser.

THE PEARL SERIES.

By MRS. MADALINE LESLIE.

Founded on, and beautifully developing the sentiment of Revelation

The Pearl Series for Boys. 6 vols. $3.00.

    PEARL OF LOVE; or, Jessie's Gift.
    PEARL OF OBEDIENCE; or, The Soldier's Son.
    PEARL OF CHARITY; or, The Chain and Seals.
    PEARL OF PATIENCE; or, Maurice and Kitty Maynard.
    PEARL OF PENITENCE; or, Charley's Sad Story.
    PEARL OF HOPE; or, The Story of Edgar.

Pearl Series for Girls. 6 vols. $3.00.

    PEARL OF FAITH; or, The Little Housekeeper.
    PEARL OF FORGIVENESS; or, Ruth Stanley.
    PEARL OF CONTENTMENT; or, Floy and her Nurse.
    PEARL OF MEEKNESS; or, Our Little Belle.
    PEARL OF DILIGENCE; or, The Basket Weavers.
    PEARL OF PEACE; or, The Little Peacemaker.

BEAUTIFUL BOOKS FOR INFANT CLASSES.

Finely Illustrated.

LITTLE ADDIE'S LIBRARY.

By COUSIN BELLE. 12 vols. $3.

. ADDIE'S COUNTRY HOME.	ADDIE'S NEW "STORY BOOK."
ADDIE'S VISITORS.	LAURA'S GARDEN.
WORKING FOR MAMMA.	THE LOST CHILD.
ADDIE'S BROTHER FREDDIE.	WORKING FOR PAPA.
ADDIE'S BIRTHDAY.	THE MAGIC LANTERN.
THE SAIL ON THE RIVER.	ADDIE'S PARTY.

LITTLE KEEPSAKE LIBRARY.

By COUSIN BELLE. 6 vols.

ADDIE'S COUNTRY HOME.	ADDIE'S VISITORS.
ADDIE'S BIRTHDAY.	ADDIE'S PARTY.
WORKING FOR MAMMA.	ADDIE'S NEW "STORY BOOK."

COUSIN BELLE'S LIBRARY.

FOR THE LITTLE FOLKS. 6 vols.

LAURA'S GARDEN.	THE LOST CHILD.
ADDIE'S BROTHER FREDDIE.	WORKING FOR PAPA.
THE MAGIC LANTERN.	THE SAIL ON THE RIVER.

WATER LILY STORIES.

Twelve volumes. 32mo. In box. $3.

THE GOLD BRACELET.	JAN HARMSEN, the Dutch Orphan.
ALICE AND HER PUPILS.	BETSY BARTLETT.
ROSE AND HER TROUBLES.	KATE AUBREY'S BIRTHDAY.
CHARLES MORTON.	PATIENCE AND HER FRIENDS.
THE LITTLE FOREST GIRL.	WILL THORNTON, the Crow Boy.
SIX-PENNY CALICO.	

THE CEDAR BROOK STORIES;
OR, THE CLIFFORD FAMILY.

By MRS. A. S. MOFFAT.   5 vols.   18mo. $3.25

LITTLE SEED SOWERS.   SEED GROWING
SEED BEARING FRUIT.   SOWING IN NEW FIELDS.
FRANK GONE TO THE WAR.

These five volumes, handsomely illustrated, in a neat box. They are by one of the best of our writers, and are every way adapted to the family or Sabbath school.

GEORGIE'S MENAGERIE.

By MRS. MADALINE LESLIE.   6 vols. $3.75.

THE LION.   THE WOLF.
THE BEAR.   THE CAMEL.
THE DEER.   THE ELEPHANT.

These six volumes are handsomely illustrated, in neat box.

A very interesting account of the life and habits of each animal described in the book is given, and much valuable information can be obtained by reading these books.

THE ARLINGTON SERIES.

4 vols.   16mo.   In box. $5.50.

ONE-ARMED HUGH.   WHEEL OF FORTUNE.
BOYS AT DR. MURRAY'S.   THE DESERTED MILL.

THE LAKESIDE STORIES.

3 vols. $4.25.

THE BROKEN PITCHER.   MABEL ROSS.
LUKE DARRELL.

THE GUNBOAT SERIES.

6 vols. $7.50.

FRANK THE YOUNG NATURALIST.
FRANK ON A GUNBOAT.
FRANK IN THE WOODS.
FRANK BEFORE VICKSBURG.
FRANK ON THE LOWER MISSISSIPPI.
FRANK ON THE PRAIRIE.

THE SUNSHINE SERIES.

By H. N. W. B. Six volumes. 18mo. $3.90. The volumes of this series are

HONEYSUCKLE COTTAGE.   TONY AND HIS HARP.
THE LITTLE FLORENTINE.   TIMMY TOP-BOOTS.
THE LOAD OF CHIPS.   SOPHIA AND THE GIPSEYS.

This is an entirely new series of books, by one of the best writers of juvenile books. They are put up in a neat box, and will be found excellent for the Sabbath School Library.

THE FERNSIDE LIBRARY.

Six volumes. Muslin. Illustrated. In a neat box. $7.50.

ANN ASH.   ANNE DALTON.
THE CONVICT'S SONS.   DON'T SAY SO.
THE ERRAND BOY.   THE TWO FIRESIDES.

THE ROSEDALE LIBRARY.

Six volumes. 16mo. Illust. In neat box. $6.

HENRY ARDEN.   HONEST GABRIEL.
JOE FULWOOD.   KATE KEMP.
LITTLE JANE.   LITTLE GERMAN DRUMMER BOY.

THE BOARDMAN LIBRARY.

By MRS. W. E. BOARDMAN. Four vols. 16mo. Illust. In a neat box. $5.

HAPS AND MISHAPS OF THE BROWN FAMILY.
THE SISTER'S TRIUMPH.
NELLY GATES AND THE LITTLE MISSIONARY.
THE MOTHER-IN-LAW.

AMY GARNETT,
One vol., 16mo. $1.25.

Mr. Graves's list of Juveniles comprises some of the best sets in the market. Full lists sent on application.

LINDA NEWTON.
By MRS. L. J. H. FROST. 16mo. $1.50.

This story is of thrilling interest, and one that can be placed into every family circle or Sabbath School, with the assurance that it will do good. The religious tone of it is superior. The purity and beauty of style is not excelled. It can but be ranked with the best.

DAVY'S MOTTO.
16mo. $1.25.

An excellent book for boys, of school life, and one that every boy will like and be profited in reading.

THE PERCY FAMILY.

By Rev. D. C. Eddy, D. D.   5 vols. Illustrated. $5.

Visit to Ireland.   England and Scotland.
Paris to Amsterdam.   Baltic to Vesuvius.
         The Alps and the Rhine.

This set of books give an account of Dr. Eddy's visit to Europe, and gives very interesting accounts of the places visited by him, and what came under his own observations. A merchant is represented taking his two children upon a European tour, and the whole is written in a manner which cannot fail of interesting the young, as well as those older in life.

One-Armed Hugh; or, the Corn Merchant. 1 vol. 16mo. $1.50.

A story of a poor boy, who accidentally lost his arm, but who was assisted by friends, not only to support himself, but a widowed mother, and to become a useful man. It is an excellent book.

The Wheel of Fortune. By Mrs. Madaline Leslie. 16mo. $1.50.

An interesting book, — showing the ups and downs of life, teaching a lesson which all should learn.

Boys at Dr. Murray's. By Glance Gaylord.

A good story of a school life, and an admirable illustration of what a perfect forgiving spirit and true friendship should be; in the case of Grant Westerley, whose noble efforts won Willett Howth, a fellow-scholar, back from disgrace, and made a man of him.

The Deserted Mill, and Potter Family. By E. L. Llewellen. 16mo. $1.25.

Joe and the Howards; or, Armed with Eyes. By Carl. 16mo. $1.25.

It gives much valuable information in regard to insects, both on land and water, in such a manner as cannot fail to amuse children, while it is storing their minds with that which is useful for them to know.

Gilbert Starr and his Lessons. By Glance Gaylord. 1 vol. 16mo. Illustrated. $1.50.

Gilbert's Last Summer at Rainford. By Glance Gaylord. 1 vol. 16mo. Illustrated. $1.50.

Will Rood's Friendship. By GLANCE GAYLORD. 1 vol. 16mo. Illustrated. $1.50.

Jack Arcombe. 1 vol. 16mo. Illustrated. $1.50.

Visit to Ireland. By REV. D. C. EDDY, D. D. 16mo. Illustrated. $1.

England and Scotland. By REV. D. C. EDDY, D. D. 16mo. Illustrated. $1.

Paris to Amsterdam. By REV. D. C. EDDY, D. D. 16mo. Illustrated. $1.

Baltic to Vesuvius. By REV. D. C. EDDY, D. D. 16mo. Illustrated. $1.

The Alps and the Rhine. By REV. D. C. EDDY, D. D. 16mo. Illustrated. $1.

Live and Learn. By MRS. LESLIE. 1 vol. 16mo. $1.25.

The Governor's Pardon. By MRS. LESLIE. 1 vol. 16mo. $1.25.

The Errand Boy; OR, YOUR TIME IS YOUR EMPLOYER'S. 16mo. Muslin. Illustrated. $1.25.

Don't Say So; OR, YOU MAY BE MISTAKEN. 16mo. Muslin. Illustrated. $1.25.

The Myrtle Stories, 1 vol. $1.75.
This is finely illustrated with a large number of engravings; also a border and title-page printed in colors, making one of the most beautiful books for the holidays published.

Behind the Curtain; OR, LELINAN THE INDIAN GIRL. 16mo. $1.25.

Helps and Hindrances to the Cross. 16mo. $1.25.

Breach of Trust; OR, THE PROFESSOR AND POSSESSOR. 16mo. $1.25.

Arabian Nights. 12mo. $1.75.

Robinson Crusoe. 12mo. $1.75.

Swiss Family Robinson. 12mo. $1.75.

The Myrtle Stories. 16mo. $1.

Anna Dai'on ; OR, HOW TO BE USEFUL. 16mo. Muslin. Illustrated. $1.25.

Convict's Son. 1 vol. 16mo. Illustrated. $1.25.

Haps and Mishaps. 1 vol. 16mo. Illustrated. $1.25.

Sister's Triumphs. 1 vol. 16mo. Illustrated. $1.25.

Two Firesides. 1 vol. 16mo. Illustrated. $1.25.

Ann Ash. 1 vol. 16mo. Illustrated. $1.25.

Mother-in-Law. 1 vol. 16mo. Illustrated. $1.25.

Nellie Gates. 1 vol. 16mo. Illustrated $1.25.

Blind Nellie's Boy. By T. S. ARTHUR. 1 vol. 16mo. $1.

Paul Barton. 16mo. $1.25.

Behind the Curtain. 16mo. $1.25.

Breach of Trust. 16mo. $1.25.

Helps and Hindrances. 16mo. $1.25.

Walter and Frank. 16mo. $1.25.

Nellie Milton's Housekeeper. 16mo. $1.25.

Brownie Sanford. 16mo. $1.25.

Sylvia's Burden. 16mo $1.25.

The Young Man's Friend. NEW SERIES. By REV. D. C. EDDY, D. D. $1.50.

This excellent book consists of a series of discourses delivered by Dr. Eddy to "Young Men," and is one which cannot fail of making a lasting impression on whoever shall read it.

The Young Man's Friend. FIRST SERIES. By REV. D. C. EDDY, D. D. $1.50.

The Heroines of the Church. By REV. D. C. EDDY, D. D. $1.50.

Angel Whispers. By REV. D. C. EDDY, D. D. $1.50.

The Hand of Jesus. By REV. J. D. CHAPLIN, D. D. 18mo; gilt. $1.50.

This is a book of devotion. It is put up in a neat form, as a gift book, and is an excellent religious book.

The Mind and Words of Jesus, AND FAITHFUL PROMISES. 18mo. 75 cents.

The Words of Jesus. 50 cents.

The Mind of Jesus. 50 cents.